Love is in the air....

A change had come over the seventh-grade wing, and Emma-Jean sensed it the moment she entered the school building the next morning. Like a flock of starlings swarming before a storm, Emma-Jean's peers were suddenly abuzz with excitement over the Spring Fling.

"What's gotten into these kids!" she heard Mr. Petrowski saying as she rounded the corner between classes. "They're out of control." He was speaking to Ms. Wright, Emma-Jean's esteemed language arts teacher.

"Oh Phil," Ms. Wright said, "love is in the air. These kids are like the birds and the bees. They've got spring fever."

Emma-Jean was intrigued by Ms. Wright's hypothesis. She thought of the joyous song of the yellow warbler outside the science room and the bees buzzing sprightly among the lilacs. Perhaps this excitement among her peers was a seasonal phenomenon.

But then she had an alarming thought: Did she have spring fever too?

OTHER BOOKS YOU MAY ENJOY

Emma-Jean Lazarus Fell in Love

Lauren Tarshis

PUFFIN BOOKS
An Imprint of Penguin Group (USA) Inc.

For Dionisia Severino

PUFFIN BOOKS
Published by the Penguin Group
Penguin Young Readers Group, 345 Hudson Street, New York, New York 10014, U.S.A.
Penguin Group (Canada), 90 Eglinton Avenue East, Suite 700, Toronto, Ontario, Canada M4P 2Y3
(a division of Pearson Penguin Canada Inc.)
Penguin Books Ltd, 80 Strand, London WC2R 0RL, England
Penguin Ireland, 25 St Stephen's Green, Dublin 2, Ireland (a division of Penguin Books Ltd)
Penguin Group (Australia), 250 Camberwell Road, Camberwell, Victoria 3124, Australia
(a division of Pearson Australia Group Pty Ltd)
Penguin Books India Pvt Ltd, 11 Community Centre,
Panchsheel Park, New Delhi - 110 017, India
Penguin Group (NZ), 67 Apollo Drive, Rosedale, North Shore 0632, New Zealand
(a division of Pearson New Zealand Ltd.)
Penguin Books (South Africa) (Pty) Ltd, 24 Sturdee Avenue,
Rosebank, Johannesburg 2196, South Africa

Registered Offices: Penguin Books Ltd, 80 Strand, London WC2R 0RL, England

First published in the United States of America by Dial Books for Young Readers,
a division of Penguin Young Readers Group, 2009
Published by Puffin Books, a division of Penguin Young Readers Group, 2010

1 3 5 7 9 10 8 6 4 2

Text copyright © Lauren Tarshis, 2009
Illustrations copyright © Kristin Smith, 2009
All rights reserved

THE LIBRARY OF CONGRESS HAS CATALOGED THE DIAL EDITION AS FOLLOWS:
Tarshis, Lauren.
Emma-Jean Lazarus fell in love / Lauren Tarshis.
p. cm.
Summary: Seventh grader Emma-Jean Lazarus uses her logical, scientific mind to navigate the
mysteries of the upcoming Spring Fling, her friend Colleen's secret admirer,
and other love-related dilemmas.
ISBN: 978-0-8037-3321-3 (hardcover)
[1. Interpersonal relations—Fiction. 2. Problem-solving—Fiction. 3. Middle schools—Fiction.
4. Schools—Fiction.] I. Title.
PZ7.T211115El 2009
[Fic]—dc22
2008046260

Puffin Books ISBN 978-0-14-241568-9

Printed in the United States of America

Designed by Teresa Dikun
Text set in New Century Schoolbook

Acknowledgments

Every day—every hour—I feel grateful for the blessings of my life, including the opportunity to be a part of the world of children's books. For this, I am deeply grateful to Lauri Hornik, whose editorial wisdom, unflagging support, and friendship have made this book a source of ongoing delight and excitement for me. I would like to thank the entire team at Dial Books, especially Mary Raymond for opening all those library doors, Kristin Smith for her beautiful Yellow Warblers, Regina Castillo for her keen editorial eye, and Shelley Diaz for all of her help. I would not be writing children's books if it were not for Gail Hochman, the finest agent a person could hope for, who offered words of encouragement way back when and whose embracing attentions would give anyone confidence. Nancy Mercado helped bring Emma-Jean into my life in 2007, and her guiding spirit remains with me. I am ever grateful to my friends and colleagues at *Storyworks* magazine, particularly Deb Dinger, who has been my beloved friend and creative partner for more than fifteen years. To Stefanie Dreyfuss, I am grateful for your friendship and daily words of support. To my parents, Karen and Barry Tarshis; my husband, David Dreyfuss; and my children, Leo, Jeremy, Dylan, and Valerie, I love you all more than I could ever express in words. And to my Nana, Jennie Ross, happy ninetieth birthday.

Chapter 1

Emma-Jean Lazarus knew very well that the seventh-grade boys at William Gladstone Middle School behaved like animals at times. They threw fruit in the cafeteria and stampeded through the hallways. They chased balls on the blacktop and laughed in a howling manner when Mr. Petrowski discussed a certain part of the digestive system in science.

But none of this particularly troubled Emma-Jean. She had been observing her fellow seventh graders for many years, trying to understand them better. And she had long ago concluded that it was simply the boys' nature to be rambunctious on occasion. She also had a compelling theory about this, which she was pleased to share with her four new friends one afternoon as they sat together in the cafeteria.

It was a bright Monday in May, and Emma-Jean had been quietly sipping her tomato soup and listening as the girls engaged in their usual lively lunchtime chatter. Already they had covered an impressive range of topics, from the wart on Kaitlin's finger to the Spring Fling, an upcoming formal dance sponsored by the PTA, for which the girls were expected to invite the boys.

After weeks of heated discussion and debate, the girls had determined that they would not attend the dance. As a festive alternative, Colleen had proposed a sleepover party, where she would serve chocolate fondue. She supplied daily updates on the status of her preparations, including today's announcement that her mother had successfully purchased a fondue pot at a tag sale.

"I just wish you would come, Emma-Jean," Colleen said, holding out a container of neatly trimmed carrot sticks to share.

"It is not possible," Emma-Jean said.

"Why not?" Valerie asked.

"My bird becomes agitated when I am not with him overnight," Emma-Jean explained, thinking fondly of Henri, her beloved parakeet, whose roomy and immaculate cage was just a few feet from her bed.

"Oh, that's so sweet," Colleen said. "Piggy was the same way."

Kaitlin, Valerie, and Michele nodded solemnly at the mention of Colleen's beloved hamster, whose untimely death five years before still haunted Colleen. But the moment of remembrance was interrupted by an eruption of hoots and bellows from the nearby boys' table. Will Keeler and his friends were engaged in a boisterous game of table hockey, in which they were using plastic knives as sticks and a chicken nugget as a puck. Apparently Brandon Mahoney had scored a point, which was now in dispute.

The girls looked on with bemusement, clucking their tongues and rolling their eyes like mothers watching their toddlers squabble over a toy truck.

"When will they grow up?" said Valerie with an indulgent sigh.

"They're really immature," Colleen said.

"Why are they so out of control?" Kaitlin asked, peering thoughtfully into a bag of popcorn as though an answer might be etched on one of the buttery kernels.

Emma-Jean didn't usually contribute to these lunchtime conversations, but now she felt she could offer some enlightening insights.

"They are trying to call attention to themselves," Emma-Jean said.

The girls looked at her with great interest.

"What do you mean?" Michele said.

"Adolescent males engage in conspicuous displays to attract the attention of females," Emma-Jean continued.

"Like when lizards puff out their necks?" Valerie said. "I saw that on *Nature.*"

"Or when roosters strut around?" Kaitlin added, rotating her shoulders and turning her neck in a rooster-like fashion.

"They're doing this for us?" Colleen said with disbelief.

"Precisely," Emma-Jean said.

"Wow," Michele said. "I never knew that."

"You're so smart, Emma-Jean," Colleen said.

Emma-Jean nodded, pleased to share her knowledge with her new friends, and to see the appreciative smiles they offered her in return.

It had only been eleven weeks since a series of most unexpected events had propelled Emma-Jean into the midst of these fine girls. Never before had Emma-Jean experienced friendship with people of her own age, and the girls had overwhelmed her at first—their flowery and fruity smells, their bright and sparkling clothing, their shrieks and giggles, their shoulders and elbows bumping against her as she walked through the hallways.

But with each passing week, Emma-Jean was more at ease. Like the moons of Jupiter, Colleen Pomerantz, Kaitlin Vogel, Valerie Rosen, and Michele Peters moved together in harmony through the chaotic universe of William Gladstone Middle School. And if

Emma-Jean did not share their exact orbit, she was very pleased nonetheless to sit with them at their lunch table.

The period was winding down, and the girls took their last sips of chocolate milk and brushed crumbs from their laps. Emma-Jean tightened the lid of her thermos and was about to stand up when Valerie leaned forward, her amber-colored eyes shining portentously.

"Okay, now I have to tell you all . . . something . . . about Jeremy. Don't get mad!"

Jeremy Alvarez was a boy with whom Valerie had gone to drama camp during the summer. Last month, for Valerie's birthday, he'd sent her a silver bracelet adorned with a large heart-shaped charm. The bracelet had been passed around the lunch table with reverent gazes and delicate fingers, as though it were the egg of an endangered bird.

"I asked him to the Spring Fling," Valerie blurted out.

"Oh my gosh!" Colleen gasped.

Nobody spoke for a moment, and the lunchtime

din of shouts and scraping chairs and clattering trays seemed very far away.

"Well," Kaitlin said, her blond, frizzy curls quivering with excitement, "maybe I'll ask Neil. He always tries to be my partner in science."

"And I could ask Leo," Michele said tentatively, eyeing Leo Daniels, who sat with his friends from the school jazz ensemble. As usual, their trays of food remained untouched as they drummed their fingers on the table and tapped their sneakers percussively against the tile floor.

The girls regarded one another gravely, like explorers about to trek through uncharted and possibly dangerous territory.

Emma-Jean was leaning forward in a state of such riveted attention that she nearly slipped off the edge of her chair.

"What about you, Coll?" Kaitlin said abruptly. "We can still do the sleepover. And who are you going to ask? There are so many boys who would die to go with you!"

All eyes settled on Colleen, who wore an alarmed expression.

"Oh . . . well . . ." Colleen stammered, blinking her eyes very rapidly. "I guess . . . but . . . only if Emma-Jean goes."

"Will you go, Emma-Jean?" Valerie asked.

"You should!" Michele said.

"Who would you ask?" Kaitlin said.

Emma-Jean's gaze was pulled, as if by magnetic force, to Will Keeler. Just then Will smiled broadly at his band of admiring friends. He had stuffed an entire orange section into his mouth, peel intact, which gave him the appearance of an ape with bright orange teeth.

The girls had followed Emma-Jean's gaze and were now looking at her in wide-eyed amazement.

"You want to go to the Spring Fling with Will Keeler?" Valerie whispered.

Emma-Jean considered the question. She disliked dances, but the idea of standing close to Will Keeler for any length of time was appealing. Despite his untidy appearance, he had a pleasing smell, like pine needles and pennies. And she knew from personal experience that Will was an honorable person.

"Perhaps," she said.

"Oh gosh, Emma-Jean," Colleen said, her hands fluttering over her heart. "You and Will?"

"Oh no," Michele said.

"He's not right for you," Valerie said.

"And what about Laura!" Kaitlin said in a fearful whisper.

The girls looked cautiously across the cafeteria at Laura Gilroy, who was standing in line at the vending machine tapping her foot, her small eyes fluttering with impatience. The girls watched Laura with a mixture of awe and fear, as one might regard a beautiful but venomous snake.

"Laura has not asked Will to the dance," Emma-Jean said.

"But she's going to!" Valerie said.

"Any second," Kaitlin said.

"She's totally in love with him," Valerie said.

"They're together," Kaitlin said. "Everyone knows that."

Emma-Jean had a different perspective on this subject. But before she could share it, a chicken nugget came soaring through the air. It bounced off Valerie's head before landing squarely on the front of Kaitlin's sweater. Laughter roared from the boys' table, where Brandon Mahoney could be seen wielding a plastic spoon like a baseball bat. Emma-Jean's friends began to simultaneously shriek and giggle at such ear-splitting decibels that nobody heard the bell ring, and Mr. Petrowski had to shoo them from the cafeteria.

Walking through the crowded halls, Emma-Jean thought about asking Will Keeler to the Spring Fling. The idea caused her heart to flutter like the wings of the hummingbird. The sensation was unsettling, but not entirely unpleasant.

Chapter 2

Colleen sat in last period science class, and she was trying really, really, really, really hard to concentrate on what Mr. Petrowski was saying about the esophagus. But she kept thinking of Noah's Ark—about all the pigs and pandas and gorillas and ladybugs and how they'd all marched two by two, two by two, two by two onto the ark. Except for the unicorn, who couldn't find a boy who liked her, so she was left behind. To drown in the flood.

Colleen was the unicorn.

All her friends had boys they liked, and they were marching with them two by two, two by two, two by two toward the Spring Fling. Except for

Colleen, who had no boy, and would be left behind to drown.

In chocolate fondue.

Colleen sighed. She looked around the room at the boys and she felt like crying. Why didn't any of them like her? Colleen was never pushy or mean. She didn't smell bad (she hoped not . . . she breathed into her hands and sniffed . . . no, just bubble gum). Okay, so she wasn't cute like Kaitlin or funny like Valerie or talented like Michele or brilliant like Emma-Jean. But when Colleen looked in the mirror, she didn't only see braces and freckles and hair that needed way more body. She saw a face that seemed friendly and nice and ready to hear your biggest secret she would never, ever tell.

Why didn't people see that? Her friends saw it, she was pretty sure. But why not the boys?

Probably because they never looked at Colleen.

And oh gosh! What about Emma-Jean? What if she really asked Will Keeler to the Spring Fling? It would be Colleen's fault, for putting Emma-Jean on the spot at lunch. Emma-Jean didn't even like dances. But now because of Colleen, Emma-Jean might actually ask Will Keeler. And what would Will say? Probably he'd laugh and say, "I would NEVER go to a dance with YOU!"

Or maybe Will wouldn't say exactly that because he wasn't mean like some people. But still, Colleen would have to explain to Emma-Jean—in the nicest possible way—that a cute basketball boy like Will with a million friends would never go to a dance with a . . . *different* kind of girl like Emma-Jean. Colleen hoped Emma-Jean would understand. Emma-Jean was a total genius, but some things she just didn't get.

Colleen thought about Emma-Jean now, the amazing way she didn't worry about what people thought of her, how she didn't notice that Brandon Mahoney made a robot face whenever she walked by, how she knew almost nothing about boys or clothes or makeup, but everything about birds and flowers.

Colleen scrunched down in her chair and looked out the classroom window. A bird was singing. She listened harder, the way Emma-Jean might listen.

It was such a pretty sound, like the sweet little song inside Colleen's ballerina jewelry box. Colleen listened more closely, until the bird seemed to be singing just for her, until she felt herself being lifted out of her chair and carried out the window, and suddenly it was like she was high up in a tree with the bird. And from way up there, the world around her looked huge, and her school looked so small, and she got this idea—a whispery, feathery idea—that one day she wouldn't be in middle school, and maybe then she wouldn't be so worried every single minute.

And she remembered that she was really lucky. It was true. She was the luckiest girl in Connecticut, or at least in the top 100. She had her incredible mom who made sure the house was totally organized and that Colleen was never late for anything. She had her amazing friends. She was getting her braces off in fourteen months. And she had just been made head of the snack committee for the St. Mary's Church youth group, which meant that she was in charge of planning Father William's birthday party, which was just three days away. Her mom had even promised to help Colleen make the cupcakes with marshmallow frosting they'd seen on their favorite cooking show. How lucky was that?

The bell rang, and Colleen floated back to her seat. She picked up her backpack, which seemed as light as a cloud. She carried her lucky bird feeling with her through the hallways, smiling at everyone she saw, even if they didn't seem to see her.

She went to her locker and opened it on the first try. On the inside of the door there was the acrostic poem Valerie had written to her last month for her birthday. Colleen loved looking at it because it was so sweet and Valerie was such a talented poet.

C *ool*
O *odles of fun*
L *ife of the party*
L *oves animals*
E *xtraordinarily*
E *xcellently*
N *ice!!!!!!*

Colleen was about to close her locker when she noticed a folded piece of paper stuck in one of the vents. She pulled it out and unfolded it.

COLLEEN—
  I THINK YOU'RE THE BEST GIRL IN THE WHOLE GRADE.
  I HOPE YOU WANT TO GO TO THE SPRING FLING.
LOVE,
SOMEONE WHO THINKS YOU'RE SO GREAT

Colleen looked around. She held on to her locker because fainting was a definite possibility. Who could have written this? Could it be that a boy . . . liked her? Was this really happening?

Maybe that bird really *had* brought her luck!

But then she looked at the note again, and another idea hit her in the head like that time her math book fell out of her locker and she almost went into a coma.

Emma-Jean had written the note. She felt sorry for Colleen because no boy liked her, and she wanted to help. Like she'd tried to help back in February, when she by accident almost ruined Colleen's life. Of course that didn't matter now. They were friends. But didn't Emma-Jean ever learn?

Colleen looked at the note again. The lucky feeling was gone. Her bird had flown away.

Chapter 3

A change had come over the seventh-grade wing, and Emma-Jean sensed it the moment she entered the school building the next morning. Like a flock of starlings swarming before a storm, Emma-Jean's peers were suddenly abuzz with excitement over the Spring Fling.

Indeed, Emma-Jean had never seen her peers in a state of such emotional agitation, not even last month, when their custodian Mr. Johannsen revealed that his handsome fifteen-year-old grandson Carl had been cast in a role on a popular television series. Laura Gilroy's reaction to that news had been particularly extreme; she had clutched her chest and gasped *"Oh my God! Oh my God!"* in a manner that caused Emma-Jean to rush to her side, prepared to administer CPR if necessary. To Emma-Jean's relief, Laura had recovered quickly, as evidenced by the robust tone in which she shouted, *"Will you back off?"* into Emma-Jean's ear.

Emma-Jean watched her peers with keen interest throughout the afternoon. Wherever she looked, girls were huddled in whispering conferences, plotting their Spring Fling strategies. Boys who ventured too close were waved away with sly smiles and gentle chiding.

"No you don't!"

"Girl talk!"

"Hey! Top secret!"

When the girls were ready to issue their invitations, they did so with surprisingly little ceremony. A few of the bolder types simply walked up to their quarries in the hallway and blurted out, "Want to go to the Spring Fling with me?" over the noise of slamming lockers and squeaking footsteps. It was in this manner that Kaitlin invited Neil Messner, who accepted with a blushing nod as his friends slapped him on the back.

More bashful girls used their friends as intermediaries; Michele hid outside the teachers' lounge while Valerie and Kaitlin cornered Leo Daniels in the doorway of the band room. He was clearly delighted with their message, though in his excitement he dropped his bass, which barely missed Valerie's foot.

Emma-Jean found the scene fascinating yet perplexing. It was as if an enchantress had stepped out of one of the fairy tale volumes in the library and waved her wand over the seventh-grade wing. Of course Emma-Jean didn't believe in anything as fanciful as fairies or magic spells; she was firmly grounded in modern scientific principles. But clearly there were mysterious forces at work. Even the teachers took notice.

"What's gotten into these kids!" she heard Mr. Petrowski saying as she rounded the corner between classes. "They're out of control." He was speaking to Ms. Wright, Emma-Jean's esteemed language arts teacher, who was filling her thermos at the water fountain.

Emma-Jean hung back, eager to hear Ms. Wright's insights. Not only was her teacher one of her closest friends, she was one of the wisest people Emma-Jean knew. Earlier in the year, when Emma-Jean was still eating lunch by herself, Ms. Wright would often pull up a chair so that they could discuss a poem they had read in class, or to share a story from her childhood in the African country of Ghana, where the breezes smelled like roasting pumpkins and acacia flowers. Ms. Wright always had expansive views on important issues.

"Oh Phil," Ms. Wright said, "love is in the air. These kids are like the birds and the bees. They've got spring fever. You remember what it was like to be young, don't you?"

Usually Mr. Petrowski dismissed statements of this nature with a jowly frown and wave of a beefy hand, but now he looked wistfully into the distance.

"I guess I do," he said.

Emma-Jean was intrigued by Ms. Wright's hypothesis. She thought of the joyous song of the yellow warbler outside the science room and the bees buzzing sprightly among the lilacs. Perhaps this excitement among her peers was a seasonal phenomenon.

But then she had an alarming thought: Did she have spring fever too? Was it communicable, like pinkeye or an intestinal virus? Perhaps this explained the fluttering of her heart that struck whenever she saw Will.

She frowned, rejecting this notion. Unlike her peers, Emma-Jean was logical to her core, not easily carried away on emotional tides or flights of fancy. And after giving the matter some serious thought, she had determined that her friends were correct: Will was not a suitable match for her.

After all, she and Will had little in common. Unlike Emma-Jean, who had an impeccable academic record, Will was a mediocre student who spent most class periods drumming his pencil on his desk and exchanging bored looks with his friends. Unlike Emma-Jean, who had far-ranging interests including nature, poetry, and the study of Hindi, Will's only passion was the sport of basketball, which Emma-Jean considered monotonous and excessively loud.

Then again, Emma-Jean and Will shared a special kinship. Earlier in the year, Will had helped Emma-Jean by throwing a pear at Brandon Mahoney when he was pestering her in the cafeteria. She in turn had come to Will's assistance by solving a vexing problem involving Mr. Petrowski, his beloved Cadillac, and some missing chocolates. Will had been very pleased with the results of Emma-Jean's efforts on his behalf. "I owe you one," he'd said to Emma-Jean not long ago. He'd put his hand on Emma-Jean's head and, like a king bestowing a title on a noblewoman, pronounced her "a good kid." Perhaps this was not the most regal title, but it was obvious that Will held Emma-Jean in high regard.

Emma-Jean puzzled over the issue of Will Keeler throughout the afternoon. It was like a complex algebra problem, with hidden integers and variables Emma-Jean couldn't quite grasp. Laura Gilroy was certainly part of the equation, though her value was hard for Emma-Jean to calculate.

Emma-Jean was quite sure that Will did not have any affection for Laura.

He dodged her in the hallways and ignored her flamboyant dance displays on the blacktop. Most striking of all was a dramatic scene that Emma-Jean had surreptitiously witnessed at the last seventh-grade dance. Emma-Jean had stepped out of the girls' room to discover Will and Laura standing together in the deserted hallway. Emma-Jean had concealed herself in an alcove and observed the scene undetected.

"So you have to dance with me," Laura had said.

"I don't dance," Will had said.

"Not even with me?" Laura had asked in an odd, babyish voice.

"Gotta go!" Will had said, rushing away and leaving Laura to mope outside the girls' room.

Oddly, none of this had dampened Laura's ardor for Will; as recently as yesterday, she had reaffirmed her plan to invite him to the Spring Fling.

"I'm just waiting for the perfect time to ask," she had said to Emma-Jean's friends, casting her proprietary gaze across the blacktop to where Will was playing basketball with his friends.

Emma-Jean now tried to imagine how Laura would

react if another girl asked Will to the dance. The image that came to mind—a snarling dog—caused Emma-Jean to blink.

No, it would not be prudent to ask Will to the Spring Fling. In fact, she should put Will Keeler completely out of her mind.

But after the final bell had sounded, Emma-Jean found herself standing outside Will's social studies class. She followed him down the hallway and to his locker, mesmerized by the reflection of the afternoon sun on his golden hair. He looked surprised when he turned and discovered her standing behind him.

"Hey, Nancy Drew," he said. He often flattered her with this reference to the fictional detective, whose powers of observation and analysis were almost as keen as Emma-Jean's.

"Hello," said Emma-Jean, her mouth strangely dry despite the drink of water she had taken just minutes before.

"Heading to a meeting of the genius club?" said Will.

"I was not aware that there was such a club at our school," Emma-Jean replied.

Will laughed and patted Emma-Jean on the head.

"You're hilarious," he said, waving good-bye as he jogged away.

Emma-Jean had not meant to be humorous—hilarity was not in her nature. But it was gratifying to make Will smile. She followed behind him, her scalp tingling from his touch, her ears echoing with his pleasing laughter.

She stood at the windows, her heart beating with alarming vigor, and watched as Will jogged to the pickup lane and hopped into his father's truck. She waited as the truck sped away, and then stood there for a few moments more, her hand resting lightly on her head, her eyes glued to the place on the pavement that Will's sneakers had last touched.

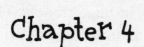

Chapter 4

Why did everything good turn bad?

That was the story of Colleen's life.

Maybe she should write a song about it, which would go something like this:

Everything good turns bad . . .
And then I get really sad.
La, la, la
La, la, la

The song was playing in her head during fourth-period Spanish when Colleen took a bathroom pass and went to flush her note down the toilet. She was standing there in the girls' room stall, all set to send the note down the drain. But then she remembered when Brandon Mahoney tried to flush his Benedict Arnold report (he'd gotten a D) and there was a flood and he got in huge trouble. That's all Colleen needed, for her note to float down the hallway for everyone to see, and besides, that wouldn't be fair to Mr. Johannsen, who would have to mop up the mess.

No, flushing wasn't the right thing to do.

She should just throw it away.

Or . . .

She could keep it.

Colleen wasn't sure.

Because even though Colleen was positively absolutely certain that Emma-Jean had written the note, there was, buried deep in her heart, the idea that maybe a boy had actually written it. That was how it always was with Colleen: No matter how sad she felt, there was always this little bit of hope—like a speck of glitter caught in your eyelash—that never went away, no matter what.

It was that tiny sparkle that made Colleen put the note back in her pocket. She kept it there for the rest of the afternoon, her secret. At the end of the day, she was supposed to go to math extra help with her friends. But instead Colleen went looking for Emma-Jean. She looked in Emma-Jean's usual hangouts, Ms. Wright's room and Mr. Johannsen's workshop and the dictionary table in the library. Finally she found her in the front lobby, staring out the windows with this fascinated look on her face, like a herd of zebras was galloping through the parking lot.

"Hey!" Colleen called, hurrying over.

"Hello," said Emma-Jean in her usual voice, like she wasn't so thrilled to see Colleen, even though Colleen had learned that this was just Emma-Jean's way, and it didn't mean anything at all, or anything Colleen had to worry about.

"Um . . . Emma-Jean . . . I have to ask you a question. Don't be surprised because it's a little . . . odd."

"I will not be surprised," Emma-Jean said. "You often ask me odd questions."

Colleen had to admit this was true. Like just

that morning in language arts, they were reading about Cyclops, the Greek mythology monster with the one huge eye, and Colleen had leaned over to Emma-Jean and whispered, "Don't I look like Cyclops?" because that morning she had woken up with the biggest pimple smack in the middle of her forehead.

She was trying to be a little funny, but Emma-Jean had stared at Colleen for what seemed like forever and then said, "Oh yes, I now see what you mean about your blemish," in her usual serious voice, which wasn't what Colleen had in mind, but what did she expect?

Colleen unfolded the note, took a deep breath, and handed it to Emma-Jean.

"So, I got this yesterday," Colleen said. "I found it in my locker. And well, I'm just wondering, did you write this, Emma-Jean?"

Emma-Jean read the note and handed it back. "No, of course I did not. My handwriting looks nothing like that."

"You didn't?"

"No," Emma-Jean repeated.

"Are you sure?" Colleen said, putting her hand on her chest because a heart attack was a definite possibility.

Emma-Jean frowned a little. "Quite sure."

Colleen threw her arms around Emma-Jean, but then let go right away because Emma-Jean wasn't the huggy type.

"Oh my gosh, Emma-Jean! You know what this means? That a boy likes me! Don't you think that's what it means? That he likes me? And he wants me to know it? And, well, the Spring Fling is coming up and I think maybe he wants me to ask him!"

Emma-Jean looked out the window and didn't say anything. For a second Colleen thought Emma-Jean had forgotten all about her, that her mind was off thinking about something Emma-Jean-ish, like tree bark or soup.

But then Emma-Jean looked back at Colleen. "Your theory is logical."

"It is?" Colleen said, not caring that her voice was all squeaky.

Emma-Jean nodded.

Colleen wanted to do a round-off back handspring, back handspring, back handspring, back flip down the hallway. But since she could barely do a cartwheel, she decided it was smarter to just jump up and down some more.

Out of all the girls in the seventh grade, a boy liked Colleen.

Colleen, who wasn't the prettiest girl in the seventh grade, or the smartest, or the funniest; Colleen, who wasn't first violin or in high math or travel soccer. A boy liked Colleen, because she was Colleen, because that was enough.

Now all she had to do was figure out who he was. And that would be a cinch!

"You'll find him for me, won't you, Emma-Jean?"

"What did you say?" Emma-Jean asked.

"You'll find out who wrote this? You'll figure it out for me!"

Of course Emma-Jean would. Because Emma-Jean was a genius. And she was Colleen's friend.

Colleen felt like singing.

Everything good doesn't always turn to bad . . .
And I'm really, really glad.
La, la, la
La, la, la

Chapter 5

Colleen was speaking loudly, and leaning in so close to Emma-Jean that her daisy and bubble-gum scent tickled Emma-Jean's nasal passages. Even so, Emma-Jean was quite certain she had misheard Colleen's question.

"You are asking for my assistance?" Emma-Jean said.

"Yes!" sang Colleen. "I am!"

Emma-Jean studied Colleen closely. "Do you not recall what happened the last time I assisted you?"

Emma-Jean remembered, in painstaking detail, how just eleven weeks earlier she had discovered Colleen sobbing in the girls' room, distraught over the news that she would not be joining Kaitlin and her family on an annual February ski trip to Vermont. For four consecutive years, Colleen had accompanied the Vogels on this trip. But this year, Laura Gilroy had used her considerable powers of manipulation to induce Kaitlin into inviting *her* instead.

Emma-Jean had attempted to assist Colleen. And her plan—carefully conceived and meticulously executed—had been successful. But it had triggered a chain reaction of unintended consequences: Laura had turned vengeful. Colleen had been overwhelmed by anguish. Emma-Jean herself had fallen out of a tree.

"Oh no!" Colleen said, waving her hand as if to erase the unpleasant images from Emma-Jean's mind. "This problem is nothing like last time. This is so simple!"

Emma-Jean knew this could not be true. If there was one thing she had learned through her close studies of her peers, it was this: Nothing was simple in the seventh grade. The most routine interactions—a joke whispered in the bus line, an offhand remark about new sneakers, a request for gum in the hallway—could turn into dramas of Shakespearean complexity, with ruthless villains, sudden plot twists, and tragic endings.

Emma-Jean was fond of her fellow seventh graders. She believed that there was no finer group of young people than the 103 boys and 98 girls with whom she shared her school days. And she was particularly pleased to have her four new friends. But her peers were irrational, and as a result, their lives were messy. In the aftermath of her fall from the tree, Emma-Jean was more determined than ever to keep out of their problems.

She opened her mouth to explain this to Colleen. But then Colleen looked at Emma-Jean in a way that conveyed that she was not exactly *asking* for Emma-Jean's help. Colleen was *expecting* Emma-Jean's help, humbly, as a flower expects the sun to shine. Colleen's eyes were wide open, filled with hope and trust. One did not often see such a look at William Gladstone Middle School.

Yet Emma-Jean had seen it before, when Colleen

and Kaitlin and Valerie and Michele caught sight of each other in the crowded hallways and hugged hello and whispered their secrets. It occurred to Emma-Jean that it was this special trusting look— more than saved seats and beaded ankle bracelets or notes signed with hearts and exclamation points— that conveyed the strength of the girls' friendship, the mysterious force that bonded them together.

Running footsteps could be heard in the hallway, and Kaitlin, Valerie, and Michele appeared around the corner.

"You won't believe what I found in my locker!" Colleen called to the girls, holding the note over her head.

The girls encircled Colleen, who held up the note for their eager eyes.

"Now do you get it? You are the best!" Kaitlin said, wrapping her arms around Colleen's shoulders and kissing her cheek.

"You have a secret admirer! You have a secret admirer!" Valerie chanted, pumping her fist into the air.

The girls smiled and swayed as though Colleen's happiness was their favorite song.

"But he won't be secret for long!" Colleen said. "Because Emma-Jean's gonna find him. Right, Emma-Jean?"

"Find him?" Kaitlin said.

The girls all looked at Emma-Jean, and she took a step closer to them.

"Yes," Emma-Jean said. "I will find him."

Chapter 6

Like a voyager returning from a faraway king-
dom, Emma-Jean walked through the front door
of her house with a grateful sigh. She enjoyed her
time at school, but after the day's excitement, she
was relieved to return to the comforting rituals of
her home.

She was greeted by a framed photograph of her
father, Eugene Lazarus, which hung on the wall
of the small entryway. He had died two years, six
months, and two days ago, in a car accident on I-95.
There was not a moment in the day when Emma-
Jean did not miss him. But very often she could
sense her father around her, his voice whispering

in the wind, his shadow dancing behind hers on a sunny day, his sparkling green eyes smiling up at her from a fresh puddle of rain. She certainly felt him in every corner of this house. She reached out and let her fingers hover over his picture. As usual he seemed to give her a reassuring nod.

Emma-Jean went to her bedroom to put away her book bag and to get Henri from his cage. Then she followed the delicious smell of sautéed garlic and curry to the kitchen to say hello to her friend Vikram Adwani, the doctoral student in immunology who rented the sunny third floor of Emma-Jean's house.

Vikram was standing at the counter, his lanky frame bent over the cutting board, his sleek black ponytail swinging rhythmically across his back as he chopped a red pepper into perfect squares. Emma-Jean was pleased to note that he was wearing the fine cotton sweater that Emma-Jean's mother had knitted him for his recent birthday. It had been Emma-Jean's idea to create a design with thirty-two stripes, one for each year of Vikram's life.

"Hello my friend," he said, smiling. "You are looking well."

"Thank you," Emma-Jean said, admiring her reflection in the shiny metal lid of Vikram's rice pot. She looked quite healthy and vigorous, no doubt due to her balanced diet and bracing daily walks to and from school.

She stood next to Vikram as he chopped, relishing his familiar kitchen sounds—the whisper of the gas flames, the gentle rattling of the simmering pots, Vikram's soft humming of a jazz melody he and Emma-Jean's mother particularly enjoyed.

Henri fluttered up from Emma-Jean's shoulder and settled on the top of Vikram's head.

"You had an interesting day at school I hope?" Vikram said, offering the bird a small square of pepper, which was accepted with an enthusiastic peck.

"Of course," replied Emma-Jean, who found every day with her peers interesting. "There is a dance coming up. It is causing a great deal of commotion among my friends."

Vikram turned and looked at Emma-Jean, his thick eyebrows raised inquisitively.

"Will you be attending?" he asked.

Emma-Jean's stomach lurched. She hesitated for just a moment before answering.

"No," she said. "I will not."

Vikram nodded as he lifted his cutting board and slid the peppers into a simmering skillet of ghee.

"I regret that I never had the opportunity to attend a dance," he said.

Emma-Jean was not surprised to hear this. There had been little money or time for recreational pursuits in the Adwani household in Mumbai, India. Vikram's parents had banked every spare rupee so that their hardworking son could realize their shared dream that he become a professor at a prestigious American university.

"Perhaps you and my mother will go to a dance," Emma-Jean said, recalling how she had recently come upon Vikram and her mother dancing together in the living room. Vikram had moved with nimble steps as her mother twirled happily around him, her tinkling laughter adding bright notes to the music playing from the stereo.

"Perhaps the three of us will have the opportunity to attend a dance together," Vikram said.

Emma-Jean and Vikram regarded each other.

It was hard to believe that it had been less than a year since Emma-Jean first met Vikram. He had responded to an advertisement Emma-Jean's mother had posted in the university housing office, seeking a responsible and quiet person to rent the sunny third floor of their home. That had been just twenty-one months after Emma-Jean's father's car accident, when even the blades of grass in their yard had seemed to tremble with grief. Vikram had moved into their home with his set of well-used pots and skillets, a voluminous library of scientific books and journals, and an air of renewal that now permeated the house like the bright scent of cinnamon.

But it was not the memory of those early days that now filled Emma-Jean's mind, but rather events surrounding a recent trip Vikram had taken to Mumbai.

The trip had come about suddenly; Vikram's mother had suffered a heart attack, and Vikram rushed to India to be by her side. Emma-Jean and her mother had driven him to the airport to catch his midnight flight.

Watching their lingering farewell embrace that night, Emma-Jean had the shocking realization that her mother had fallen in love with Vikram, and he with her. Emma-Jean had been deeply troubled by this, believing that her mother could have just one love of her life: Emma-Jean's father.

But ten days later, on the morning of Vikram's return, with the late-winter sun streaming through the windows and her mother's laughter ringing through the house, Emma-Jean realized she had been wrong. A person could have more than one love in their lifetime. And if there was anyone in this world worthy of her mother's love, surely it was Vikram Adwani.

"I believe we will do many things together," Emma-Jean said now to her friend.

"I believe you are correct," Vikram said.

Chapter 7

After wishing Vikram luck with his culinary endeavors, Emma-Jean went up to her room and sat down at her meticulous desk, which overlooked the dogwood tree she and her father had planted the spring before his accident. Henri fluttered to her shoulder and rested his velvety head against her cheek. Emma-Jean smiled, relishing one of her favorite parts of the day. Normally she would spend a sunny afternoon like this sketching the dogwood, which was in full bloom, or teaching Henri some words in Hindi.

But today there were pressing matters to attend to. She retrieved Colleen's note from the zippered compartment of her schoolbag, carefully unfolded it, and studied it closely.

The paper itself was of the lined, three-hole variety that filled practically every binder at the school. The words were written in blue ballpoint pen. To the untrained eye, the note was no more remarkable than the scraps of paper Mr. Johannsen swept into his dustbin each afternoon.

But Emma-Jean's eyes were honed from her years of observing. She knew that despite its humble appearance, this note, like a carved stone tablet unearthed from an ancient tomb, held mysteries from another world. And if the rites and rituals of seventh-grade boys were not as magnificent as those of Egyptian pharaohs and Roman emperors, they were just as intriguing to Emma-Jean.

And of course there was Colleen, a cheerful and generous girl most worthy of admiration. Emma-Jean could picture Colleen right now, sitting on her flowered bedspread, surrounded by her artfully arranged pink pillows and stuffed pigs, wearing her fluffy purple slippers and an expression of hopefulness. Suddenly the note in Emma-Jean's hands felt heavier than it should, as though the paper itself were weighted with Colleen's expectations, and Emma-Jean's trepidations. What if Emma-Jean was not successful? What if, once again, she disappointed Colleen?

Emma-Jean closed her eyes and cleared these thoughts from her mind, replacing them with the bearded and bespectacled image of Jules Henri Poincaré, the legendary French mathematician who had been her father's hero. Like Emma-Jean, the Frenchman had suffered setbacks in his problem-solving career, and yet he had never lost his optimism and his faith in the powers of creativity and logic to unlock the mysteries of the universe. Of course, Poincaré had studied celestial mechanics and chaos theory, not the relationships of seventh graders. But still, Emma-Jean felt the comparison was valid.

With renewed resolve, Emma-Jean opened her desk drawer and took out her father's magnifying glass. The carved wooden handle felt warm, as though just moments before, her father had been holding it in his hand, peering at a bat skeleton or the underside of a mushroom cap.

She examined the paper through the glass, scanning slowly until she discovered an important clue. At the bottom of the paper were oily spots, tinted pale yellow, each made up of faint swirling circles; fingerprints, of course, very likely from food residue. It seemed the author had eaten an oily snack—a cheese-powdered chip or puff of some kind—and failed to wash his hands before writing the note. This was not surprising, given the poor personal hygiene endemic among the seventh-grade boys.

Another noteworthy detail was the odd squared-off shape of the index finger. Most likely the shape represented some sort of bandage. Perhaps the author had recently suffered a splinter or paper cut.

Emma-Jean put down the magnifying glass to record these observations in her notebook. But she paused as she wrote, struck by the position of her hand on her paper, how she used the four fingers of her left hand to hold her paper steady as she wrote with her right. If Emma-Jean's fingertips had been coated with an oily, yellow food substance, her own paper would be stained like Colleen's note. But there was one critical difference. From the rise and fall of the fingers on Colleen's note, Emma-Jean could see that the author had been holding the paper down with his right hand, not his left.

The author of the note was left-handed.

A surge of excitement came over Emma-Jean as the implications of this discovery became clear. Only ten percent of the human population is left-handed, which meant that out of the 103 boys in the William Gladstone seventh grade, only approximately ten could have written this note. It occurred to Emma-Jean, not quite incidentally, that this group did not include Will Keeler, who scrawled his barely legible script and performed his much-lauded basketball layup with his right hand.

Emma-Jean contemplated her next steps. Tomorrow she would identify the left-handed boys in the seventh grade. She would study their fingers for bandages and their lunch trays for bags of fried snacks. Of course she would be alert for longing looks cast in Colleen's direction and suspicious activity in the vicinity of her locker.

Emma-Jean sat back in her chair with a feeling of satisfaction. Henri regarded her with his onyx-bead eyes.

"I have made excellent progress," she told him, scratching him gently behind the head.

Indeed, her work had progressed more quickly than she had anticipated, and there was still time to sketch the dogwood tree.

But as she reached for her sketchbook, her hand went instead to her William Gladstone sixth-grade yearbook. Without exactly meaning to, she turned to page forty-two, where Will Keeler looked sleepily out from the right-hand corner. Emma-Jean studied the picture carefully. Once again, she experienced the odd fluttering in her heart.

What could it mean?

Emma-Jean wondered about this for some time. When she looked up from Will's picture, she was astonished to discover that more than thirty minutes had passed. The dogwood tree was in shadow, and Henri was dozing contentedly on her shoulder. Emma-Jean closed the yearbook, gripped by a growing sense of alarm.

Something was happening to her, something that made no sense at all.

Chapter 8

Colleen was lying in her bed, smiling in the dark, thinking about how fun it would be to go to the Spring Fling with her boy. She thought about the dress she would wear—Long? Short? Sparkly? Twirly?—and if her mom would let her wear heels.

Oh, but her boy wouldn't care about her shoes, would he? No, Colleen decided. Her boy wasn't like that. He wouldn't care if her hands got sweaty and she stepped on his feet when they danced. Her boy would just be happy that they were together.

Colleen turned over and smiled into her pillow. Thinking about her boy gave Colleen this new feeling. It wasn't that she felt like a different person. It was the opposite of that. She felt like herself, only more—taller, braver, stronger . . .

Colleen-er.

Maybe this was how a peach felt when it was ripe, or how a brownie felt when it was all baked and ready to come out of the oven.

Even her mom had noticed the change.

"Is something going on?" her mom had asked when they were sitting in the den after dinner. Colleen was doing math and her mom was sewing Joseph and Mary sock puppets for her Sunday school class.

"Why are you asking that?" Colleen said, scared that maybe her mom had figured out that Colleen was putting on a little eye shadow when she got to school every morning. She'd wiped it off coming home on the bus, but maybe today she'd missed a spot.

"You're just acting different," her mom said, putting down her needle and reaching over to rest her hand on Colleen's cheek, like she was checking for a fever. "Are you feeling all right?"

Colleen wanted to burst out in giggles. She was so much more than all right! She wanted to tell her mom about the note and her boy and the bird, how if you wished hard enough, anything could happen.

But her mother wasn't a wishes-and-giggles type of person. Maybe she kind of used to be, when Colleen's dad lived with them. But that was so long ago, Colleen couldn't be sure.

"I'm doing fine, Mommy," Colleen said. "I'm really, really good."

And her mom seemed satisfied with that. She'd even smiled a little and nodded and said, "That's nice."

Colleen snuggled under her blanket and tried to fall asleep, but it was no use. She was too excited. And so finally she got up and sneaked across the hall to the guest room to call Kaitlin. That was one of the great things about having a best friend like Kaitlin. You could call her anytime, even at 9:50 on a Tuesday night.

"What's wrong?" Kaitlin said in a worried voice.

"Nothing!" Colleen said. "I just couldn't sleep."

"Why not?" Kaitlin said.

"I'm just so happy, you know. . ." And then she just talked and talked and talked, about her boy and the note and how romantic it was, like *Romeo and Juliet* minus the dying at the end.

"Isn't it so amazing?" Colleen said, closing her eyes, waiting for Kaitlin to exclaim, "Yes! It's the best!"

But instead Kaitlin said, "Coll, it's just a note," which made a balloon inside Colleen go *pop.*

"What do you mean?" said Colleen.

"I'm saying you shouldn't make this note into such a huge thing. So many boys like you, Coll! You need to just pick one and ask him to the Spring Fling. That's what everyone else did."

As always, Kaitlin sounded so sure, like when she was spelling a word or showing where Brazil was on a globe. Usually Colleen would just say *okay, you're right,* even if she was pretty sure Brazil was nowhere near Japan.

But not this time.

"I would never do that!" Colleen said.

"Why not?"

"Because I want to find the boy who likes me!" she said.

"All the boys like you," Kaitlin answered, which was really sweet but not true.

"But the boy who wrote this note *really* likes me! And Emma-Jean is going to help me—"

"Colleen!" Kaitlin interrupted. "Don't you remember what happened the last time Emma-Jean *helped* you?"

She said *helped* in a mean Laura Gilroy way, like Emma-Jean was a big joke.

Colleen didn't say anything. The phone felt hot in her hand. She could picture Kaitlin with her eyebrows all smooshed together, twisting one of her curls around and around and around on her finger.

Was this a fight?

Colleen wasn't sure because she never fought with her friends. Never. Not even when Kaitlin invited *Laura* to go skiing instead of Colleen, and Colleen had been so hurt. Even then, Colleen had said, "Don't worry!"

But this time Colleen couldn't just back down. This was about her boy!

"For once something really great has happened to me," Colleen said. "Can't you be happy?"

"Oh Coll . . ." Kaitlin said. "I just want *you* to be happy."

"Then be excited, okay?" She could hear her mom moving around downstairs and she needed to hurry back to bed. "Please?"

"Okay," Kaitlin said, but she still didn't sound sure.

"Love you," Colleen said.

"Me too," Kaitlin said. "You know that, right?"

"Of course!" Colleen answered.

Colleen said good-bye to Kaitlin. She felt better. She couldn't blame Kaitlin for worrying. But this wasn't like the last time Emma-Jean helped. And anyway, Colleen was so much Colleen-er now. Whatever happened, she could handle it.

Colleen went back to her room, but instead of getting into bed, she stood at her window and looked at the sky, which was so beautiful. Stars really did twinkle, just like in the song. Why hadn't Colleen ever noticed before? Probably her boy noticed. Probably

he was standing at his window right now, staring at
the sky, thinking about Colleen, who would find him
soon.

    La, la, la
    La, la, la

Chapter 9

After the dinner dishes were done and the floors were swept clean, Emma-Jean and her mother retreated to Emma-Jean's mother's bed to read and review the day's events. It was a nightly ritual that began in the days following Emma-Jean's father's accident, when the bed had seemed like a tiny raft on a vast and turbulent sea. These waters had calmed in recent months, but neither Emma-Jean nor her mother was eager to give up their cozy evening routine.

Her mother had scarcely settled her head back on the pillows when Emma-Jean began telling her about Will Keeler. Her mother listened closely as Emma-Jean described in great detail the commotion of the Spring Fling and the frenetic vibrations of her heart whenever she saw Will.

"It is clear that Will is not suitable for me in any way," Emma-Jean said. "And yet I find myself thinking about him even when I want to be thinking about other things."

Indeed, she could not recall a single fact from her classes that day. She had concluded, however, that the arrangement of freckles on Will's forearm closely resembled the constellation Virgo.

"Could it be," Emma-Jean asked, her tone grave, "that I am suffering from spring fever?"

Her mother leaned close to Emma-Jean. A spiral of auburn hair had sprung free from its barrette, and it tickled Emma-Jean's nose. It was a moment before her mother spoke.

"It is possible," she said.

Emma-Jean sat back in her pillows and put her hand to her chest.

"But it is nothing to be concerned about," her mother said, her voice briskly reassuring. "It is completely normal. It sounds like you might have a crush on Will."

"A crush?" Emma-Jean said. This sounded very serious. She pictured a boa constrictor wrapped around the neck of a lemur.

"An infatuation," her mother clarified.

"Is it the same as being in love?" asked Emma-Jean warily.

Her mother weighed the question, her eyes drifting over to her nightstand, where two framed photographs stood atop a neat stack of novels, financial reports from her job at the bank, and a Hindi dictionary she'd borrowed from Emma-Jean.

There was their favorite picture of Emma-Jean's father, smiling as he held a newborn Emma-Jean in his arms. And there was a newer photograph that Vikram had given to her, of himself as a young boy wearing the cricket uniform of his championship team.

"No," she said. "Being in love is one of the most powerful experiences anyone can have. I think that's why we have crushes when we're younger. Maybe it's how we get ready for real love."

This seemed logical to Emma-Jean. After all, many

important life skills—walking, talking, cooking, identifying birds in flight—were learned in stages and honed through practice.

"Have you ever had a crush on someone?" asked Emma-Jean.

"Absolutely," her mother said. "Several times. Haven't I told you about James Dean and me?"

Emma-Jean shook her head. She remembered the names of everyone important in her mother's life, and was quite sure that her mother had never mentioned a gentleman friend named James Dean.

"When I was about your age—maybe just a bit older—I was home sick from school and I watched a movie on TV, *Rebel Without a Cause*. And, well . . ." Her mother put a hand up to her heart. "That's when I met James Dean."

"He came to visit you?" said Emma-Jean, wondering what she would do if Will came to visit her when she was sick in bed. Perhaps he would bring her some chicken soup, though hopefully he would leave it in the kitchen so he would not be exposed to her germs.

"No, no," her mother said. "He was an actor, in the movie."

"And you knew him?"

Her mother shook her head.

"He died a good twenty years before I was even born. But that didn't matter. I was captivated. For weeks he was all I thought about." Her mother closed her eyes and smiled dreamily.

Emma-Jean considered this information. She wondered if several months before she herself had experienced a crush on George Washington. She had studied him with her social studies class, and had been deeply impressed by his forbearance during the battle of Trenton. For some weeks after, she had carried a one-dollar bill in her sweater pocket, taking it out regularly to admire the founding father's dignified gaze and impressive pompadour.

"Is there a cure for spring fever?" Emma-Jean said.

Her mother shook her head.

Emma-Jean sighed.

"Would you like my advice?" her mother said.

"I always want your advice."

"Whether or not you decide to ask Will to the dance, enjoy the experience. Because here's the big difference between being in love and having a crush: Love endures, but a crush doesn't. A crush comes on suddenly and then poof—it's gone."

"Like hives?" Emma-Jean said, recalling the time she had developed a rash after consuming a large quantity of shrimp.

Her mother smiled slightly and brushed a piece of hair from Emma-Jean's forehead.

"I'd say it's more like a dream," her mother said.

Emma-Jean looked closely at her mother. Though she was younger than the mothers of most of Emma-Jean's peers, her eyes crackled with the wisdom of a tribal elder. Emma-Jean knew she could have confidence in her mother's diagnosis: that these feelings for Will were part of a temporary condition. They would subside on their own, without outside intervention.

And in the meantime, perhaps Emma-Jean would find a way to enjoy the experience.

Chapter 10

Searching for a secret admirer in the seventh-grade wing was like tracking a great horned owl in the Connecticut woods. Both were skittish creatures, prone to flight. At no time could Emma-Jean allow the secret admirer to detect that somebody was on his trail.

She had come to school with the names of all of the seventh-grade boys written in her notebook. Throughout the morning, she observed the boys in her classes, noting R or L next to their names as they wrote in their notebooks and lab journals and calculated the volumes of irregular polygons.

The boys with whom she did not share classes

posed a bigger challenge. She could not easily observe them in the act of writing, nor could she simply approach them in the hallway and bluntly ask if they were left-handed, which could arouse suspicion. It was thus necessary to devise a clever ruse, a strategy for obtaining the needed information without signaling her motives.

"I am working on a survey," she explained to the boys when she stopped them at their lockers or outside the boys' room. "I am investigating the statistical probability of left-handedness among adolescent boys."

Of course the boys did not question the notion that Emma-Jean would be working on such an important-sounding research project. They readily provided her with the information she requested. A few also laughed heartily. This pleased her, as it wasn't often that she had the opportunity to spread mirth through the seventh-grade wing. She was happy to contribute to the positive morale in the school.

Her work went so smoothly that this phase of the project was complete before lunch. There were nine left-handed boys in the seventh grade. None of them had bandages or visible wounds on their right index finger, and while this would make Emma-Jean's job more difficult, she was relieved that the author's wound had apparently healed. Emma-Jean's friends were waiting for her at their table, and before she could even pull out her chair, they were barraging her with questions.

"Why were you talking to those boys after math?" asked Michele.

"I bet you know exactly who it is!" Valerie exclaimed, bouncing in her chair.

"You found him, didn't you?" said Colleen.

Emma-Jean sat down and took out her thermos. "I have not yet completed my investigation," she said.

"I told you she wouldn't know," Kaitlin said, shaking her head at Valerie.

"But you have some idea, Emma-Jean," Valerie said, eyeing Kaitlin with annoyance. "Don't you?"

Emma-Jean now found herself in a delicate position. She could certainly understand her friends' curiosity. But to reveal anything now was risky. While her friends would never intentionally undermine her investigation, they were loquacious by nature, trading intimacies as casually as they shared lip gloss and breath mints. Any details Emma-Jean disclosed could quite possibly get back to the secret admirer, with disastrous results.

"I am sorry," Emma-Jean said. "All information pertaining to this project is confidential."

"We would never tell a soul!" Michele said.

"You can trust us," Colleen said.

"We know how to keep secrets," Valerie said, making a zipper-like motion over her tightly closed lips.

They continued to question and cajole in such an insistent manner that Emma-Jean lost her appetite. Her thermos sat before her unopened, as though it too had secrets it could not divulge. As the pleading persisted, Emma-Jean thought of the hungry mallards that followed her and her mother along the riverbank, flapping their wings and quacking frantically for bread crusts.

Perhaps a few crumbs of information would satisfy her friends' ravenous curiosity.

"All right," Emma-Jean said in a low voice. "I will

tell you that I have made an important discovery."
She looked over her shoulder for eavesdroppers, and
then said in a low voice, "The boy who wrote the note
is left-handed."

"Oh my gosh!" Colleen said, clasping her hands to
her heart. "Everyone knows left-handed boys are the
most romantic!"

"But how can you tell he's left-handed?" Kaitlin
asked.

"I examined the note under magnification,"
Emma-Jean explained. "I discovered fingerprints on
the paper, and from their placement I deduced that
he is left-handed."

"What's deduced?" Michele said.

"It's guessing," Kaitlin said.

"No it's not," Valerie said.

"A deduction is a conclusion drawn through logic,"
Emma-Jean clarified.

"Wow," Michele and Valerie chorused, shaking
their heads with awe.

"Aren't there a lot of left-handed boys?" Kaitlin
said.

"Only one in ten people in the world is left-handed," Emma-Jean said. "I have discovered that there are nine in our seventh grade."

"That's all?" Valerie said, grabbing Colleen's hands. "And one of them is in love with you!"

"That's a lot," Kaitlin said. "And there could be more."

"Kaitlin, stop being so negative!" Valerie scolded. "You're ruining all the fun!"

"This isn't a game, Valerie," Kaitlin said in an aggrieved tone. "This is Colleen's life! And don't blame me for not wanting her to be totally devastated if this doesn't work out how she wants!"

All eyes turned to Colleen, who was indeed the most fragile of the girls, easily upset by even the most benign conflicts. A recent debate about soda flavors had caused Colleen to put her hands over her ears and implore, "Can't we all just agree?"

But now Colleen sat tall, her face serene. She did not look any different, with her long neck and neatly combed bangs and spray of freckles across her upturned nose. But she seemed changed somehow, more distinct and illuminated, as though there was a bright light shining out from behind her large turquoise eyes. Perhaps she was taking vitamins, Emma-Jean thought, or eating more leafy vegetables.

It was Kaitlin who appeared agitated, her cheeks blotchy and flushed, her curls askew.

"You don't have to worry about me," Colleen said, putting her arm around Kaitlin. "No matter what, I'll be okay."

"But what about Emma-Jean?" Kaitlin said. "She's totally stressed out. It's too much pressure. I mean, look at her!"

The girls leaned forward to inspect Emma-Jean, who did her best to maintain her usual unperturbed expression.

"She looks gorgeous," Colleen pronounced. "As usual."

Kaitlin opened her mouth to comment, but the sound of Laura Gilroy's voice called their attention to the other side of the cafeteria.

"Come on, lazy butts," Laura called, pointing in their direction and shaking her hips, the dreaded signal that it was time for the girls to report to the blacktop for a dance rehearsal. The girls did not enjoy these sessions, during which Laura bullied and belittled them as they attempted to follow her complex choreography of shimmies and kicks. And Emma-Jean knew they did not relish Laura's company. They complained about her when she was out of earshot, and quietly rejoiced when she failed a pop quiz in language arts or split her pants performing a particularly showy leap.

But for some reason they admired Laura, and feared her. And now, like dutiful soldiers, they rose out of their chairs.

Colleen lingered as the other girls returned their trays and disappeared out the back door.

"I hate dancing with Laura," Colleen sighed.

"I know you do," Emma-Jean said, which caused Colleen to smile.

"You know everything about me, don't you, Emma-Jean?" Colleen said.

"Not everything," said Emma-Jean, who would never presume to have total knowledge of any subject.

"Well, I know some things about you too," Colleen said. "And one thing I know for sure is that you're a really good friend."

"Thank you," Emma-Jean said, surprised by the compliment. Emma-Jean had many areas of expertise—geometry and watercolor painting and the flora and fauna native to Connecticut. But her knowledge of friendship was still rudimentary. Colleen, on the other hand, was an expert.

Kaitlin appeared at the back door of the cafeteria, and began calling to Colleen and waving her arms.

"Colleen!" Kaitlin called. "Laura's waiting!"

"Coming!" Colleen replied, hoisting her backpack onto her back and grabbing her tray. She paused for a moment, leaning in close to Emma-Jean.

"I just have this feeling," she said, her voice rich with portent. "I think amazing things are going to happen, for both of us. I just feel . . . if you really believe in your heart, then anything is possible, you know?"

And then she scurried off.

Emma-Jean was dumbstruck by Colleen's words,

for they reminded her of her father's favorite quote by Poincaré,

It is by logic that we prove, but it is in the heart that we discover life's possibilities.

The meaning of those words had perplexed Emma-Jean. The heart, after all, was simply a muscle. It could not observe or analyze. One could not look inside one's own heart without the use of sophisticated machinery. And even then, what would one discover other than four chambers pulsing with blood?

But now Emma-Jean considered her own heart. Were there possibilities waiting to be discovered? How could she know?

These questions troubled Emma-Jean. But then she was struck by an intriguing notion: that her heart was like a poem.

She thought of the poems she often discussed with Ms. Wright, and how she had learned to look beyond simple words and fanciful rhymes to discover hidden meanings, profound ideas about life and death.

And just as Emma-Jean had learned to understand poetry, she believed, she would someday learn to read her own heart.

At that moment, Will Keeler went careening by on his way out to the blacktop, and the sight of him sent Emma-Jean's heart into its predictable frenetic rhythms.

She wondered if Poincaré had experienced a crush when he was young.

Probably yes, Emma-Jean thought, though she doubted that the object of the Frenchman's affections had chocolate milk stains on her shirt.

Chapter 11

Just because Colleen was busy with her boy didn't mean that she could forget about her other important responsibilities, like her position as the head of the St. Mary's youth group snack committee. Tonight was Father William's birthday party, and she had to be focused.

This morning, she and her mom had gotten up at 5:00 to make four dozen chocolate marshmallow cupcakes. And this afternoon, Colleen would go to the church to get everything ready. Kaitlin had promised to help her. They had been talking all week about how they would arrange the flowers and balloons and set up the food table so it looked like a page out of one of Colleen's mom's magazines. Colleen would never want to brag, but she and Kaitlin were really talented at arranging baked goods. Maybe they'd start a business one day.

But just as Colleen and her mom were walking out the front door, the phone rang, and it was Kaitlin saying, "I'm not coming."

Colleen couldn't believe it!

"You have to come!" Colleen said, but Kaitlin kept saying she wasn't in the mood, and finally Colleen's mom went outside and started the car, and Colleen had to go.

She hung up in shock.

How could Kaitlin just call her and cancel, like Father William's party was an orthodontist appointment? And how could Colleen be at the party by herself?

Because this wasn't a regular youth group party. Other kids from church were coming, kids who never came to youth group, like Will Keeler, whose dad had donated the rose bush they were planting in Father

William's honor, and Brandon Mahoney, who followed Will everywhere.

What if Will and Brandon turned the party into a huge joke? What if they thought youth group was for dorks? What if Brandon made up a mean name for Colleen, like rotten cookie Colleen or gross snack Colleen . . . Colleen wasn't good at making up mean names, but Brandon was a genius at it. It was Brandon who thought of the name Emma-Jean Spaz-arus. And a few months back he had drawn a picture of a really fat man on Mr. Petrowski's blackboard with the words *Mr. Pigtrowski* written under it.

Oh gosh! What would Colleen do?!

She had to get the party ready, that was for sure. She loved Father William and would never want to disappoint him. But maybe she could get everything perfect and then call her mom and say that she felt dizzy and that her stomach hurt. It wouldn't be a lie because even thinking about the party was making Colleen's head spin and her stomach twist.

And so that was Colleen's plan.

Her mom dropped Colleen and the cupcakes off

at the church. Colleen worked by herself to set up the room so it looked really gorgeous. By 6:30 she was finished, and there was still half an hour before the party, plenty of time for her mom to come and pick her up.

She started walking to the church office to use the phone.

But wait . . .

Suddenly she didn't feel like she was all alone.

She looked around, and there was nobody with her in the room. But she had this feeling that someone was right there, watching over her, and not in the creepy horror movie way.

Her boy. That's who it was.

He seemed to be right there with her. And he was reminding her that she'd been so excited about this party, and that not even Brandon Mahoney would be mean on Father William's birthday.

Colleen took a deep breath. The room looked amazing and Father William would be so happy.

And with her boy close by, Colleen didn't have to worry about a thing.

Chapter 12

Dinner was always a notable affair at Emma-Jean's house due to the superb meals Vikram created. But this evening was especially festive because of a special guest: Ms. Wright.

Emma-Jean had long suspected that her language arts teacher would fit in well at their dining table, and her instinct had been correct. Since their first meal together in March, Ms. Wright had developed a close kinship with Emma-Jean's mother and Vikram, and a long list of favorites from Vikram's culinary repertoire.

As usual, the animated conversation began the moment Ms. Wright entered the house with her radiant smile. Ms. Wright stood in the kitchen with Emma-Jean's mother while Emma-Jean chopped cilantro and zested lemons for Vikram's final flourishes. At one point Ms. Wright leaned over the pot of simmering chicken korma and inhaled deeply.

"Heaven," she sighed. "That's all there is to say."

They took their seats at the table, and Ms. Wright admired a large bowl, which Emma-Jean's parents had purchased while on their honeymoon in Turkey.

"I need a nice serving bowl like that," Ms. Wright said. "I'm having a friend over this Saturday, and I have nothing really lovely to serve with."

"Someone we know?" Emma-Jean's mother asked as she offered Ms. Wright a dollop of pineapple chutney.

"You must know Phil Petrowski," Ms. Wright said.

"Of course," Emma-Jean's mother said, her eyebrows raised in surprise. "The science teacher. I didn't realize you were friends."

"We have our differences," Ms. Wright said. "But

lately I've come to appreciate Phil. He's a good man, a very good man."

"Will this be a romantic evening?" Vikram asked delicately.

A chickpea fell off of Emma-Jean's fork, as though Vikram's shocking suggestion had caused it to faint. Was it possible that the graceful and enlightened Ms. Wright was in love with the blustery Mr. Petrowski, whose main passion was his red Cadillac Escalade?

If this was true, Emma-Jean knew even less about love than she had feared.

"No, nothing like that," Ms. Wright said. "Last week I was mentioning that I loved fresh tomatoes, and on Sunday afternoon he stopped by with a tomato plant to plant in my yard. I said to him, 'Phil, if I were twenty years younger, I'd have to marry you.' We had a good laugh over that one. Anyway, I'm going to make him a nice dinner, to thank him. I think he's . . . maybe a little lonely."

Emma-Jean had never stopped to consider Mr. Petrowski's life outside of the seventh-grade wing. And now it saddened her to think that he went home each afternoon to an empty house. Perhaps she could suggest to him that he purchase a parakeet, like Henri, who could say hello in English, Spanish, French, and Hindi.

"Has Mr. Petrowski ever been married?" asked Emma-Jean's mother.

"No," Ms. Wright said. "I suppose he never found the right person."

"That's a shame," said Emma-Jean's mother as Vikram gazed at her.

"Maybe he could still find someone," said Emma-Jean.

Ms. Wright nodded. "Of course," she said.

Emma-Jean hoped so.

"And what about you?" Emma-Jean's mother said to Ms. Wright.

This was a sensitive subject for Emma-Jean, for not long ago she was quite certain she had found the perfect match for Ms. Wright: Vikram. Of course, that was before Emma-Jean discovered that Vikram was in love with her mother. She still hoped to find a suitable match for her esteemed teacher.

"I don't think you need much help in that area," Emma-Jean's mother continued, smiling at Ms. Wright.

"That's very nice of you to say," Ms. Wright said. "The truth is that I am very content as things are. I'm not really looking."

"It would not be easy to find someone for you," Emma-Jean said.

Ms. Wright looked surprised.

"Why is that?" Emma-Jean's mother asked.

"Because few men are worthy of Ms. Wright."

Ms. Wright smiled. "Is that so?"

"Yes," Emma-Jean said. "It is."

"Well, no pressure. But if you happened to find an intelligent man out there with a good sense of humor and a love of music, you can send him my way."

Emma-Jean's mother raised her glass. "To music and laughter," she said, and they all tapped their glasses together with a most satisfying *clink*.

Chapter 13

Even with her boy right there beside her, Colleen felt pretty nervous as the party got started, especially when Father William told everyone to huddle up.

"Let's give a hand to Colleen for putting together this beautiful gathering," he said. "Colleen, you put your heart into this like you always do, and it shows."

Usually Colleen felt totally embarrassed when Father William singled her out. Her cheeks would get bright red and she'd try to hide behind Kaitlin until people stopped clapping and staring.

This time, though, her boy wouldn't let her hide. He gave her a little nudge toward Father William, and told her to smile and enjoy this moment.

And the most amazing thing happened a little later, when Colleen was neatening up the platters on the snack table.

"Those look awesome," said a familiar boy's voice behind her.

Was that Will Keeler? Talking to Colleen?

Colleen turned around and there he was, looking at her and pointing at the chocolate marshmallow cupcakes, which did look really delicious.

"Who made these?" he said.

Colleen's head popped off and flew into the air, but her boy caught it and put it back on her neck. She took a deep breath. She never talked to Will or any of the boys. There were so many times she'd wanted to talk to them, when she thought of something fascinating to say, like "How long is your bus ride?" or "Don't you think the cafeteria should get strawberry milk?" But then she would get nervous that her voice would sound all squeaky or that the boy would walk away without answering.

But now when Colleen looked at Will, she didn't see the handsome thirteen-year-old basketball boy.

She saw cute little Willy K. from nursery school, with the yellow curls and tow truck T-shirt. She remembered how he used to hug his mom so tightly when she said good-bye at drop-off. Probably Will was still the same sweet boy now that he was then, only with hairier arms and bigger muscles.

"*I* made those," Colleen said. "My mom and me."

"They look good."

"They are," Colleen said.

Who said that? Was that really Colleen Julianna Pomerantz talking? Oh gosh, was she bragging?

"Really?" Will said, smiling at her.

Will looked at her right in the eyes. And if Colleen hadn't been totally in love with her boy, she would have thought that Will Keeler was the dreamiest boy she'd ever seen, or ever would see for as long as she lived.

No wonder Laura was in love with him! And Emma-Jean too!

Will picked up a cupcake and took a big bite. He chewed very slowly, watching Colleen. He swallowed in a cartoony way, which was really funny. Colleen laughed, and her laugh didn't sound squeaky. It sounded normal and funny, like she was an actress on TV playing the part of a girl with a good laugh.

"Those are the best cupcakes I've ever tasted."

"Thank you!" Colleen said.

And just like that, Will Keeler and Colleen were friends. Colleen knew how that could be, how one funny little moment—like a tiny drop of superglue— was enough to stick two people together. Moments like that were really precious, Colleen knew, because she'd had some with all of her friends. She collected them, memorizing every detail. Sometimes in bed, she'd play these memories back in her mind, tiny movies that would lull her happily to sleep.

Just then someone slapped Will on the back so hard he almost fell face-first into a Bundt cake.

Brandon Mahoney!

"There you are!" he said to Will.

Brandon grabbed one of Colleen's cupcakes and stuffed the whole thing into his mouth.

"Mmmmm," he said.

"Colleen made those," Will said.

Brandon picked up another one.

"I guess Brandon likes them," Will said.

"I guess so," Colleen said.

"You know what your new name is?" Brandon said with frosting all over his teeth.

Uh-oh.

Brandon licked his fingers. "From now on, I'm gonna call you . . ."

Colleen held her breath.

"Collcakes," Brandon said.

Wait. Was that so bad?

"Know why?" Brandon said.

"Because she's sweet?" Will said.

"Yep," Brandon said.

And Brandon laughed, and Colleen laughed, and Will laughed, and Colleen's boy laughed too.

La, la, la

La, la, la

La, la, la, la, la

Chapter 14

As usual, their evening with Ms. Wright continued long after they'd eaten the last of the chicken and rice. They debated the day's headlines and critiqued their favorite films. Emma-Jean and Ms. Wright recited their favorite Mary Oliver poem, about gathering peonies in the early morning, and Vikram shared a most humorous story about his high school cricket team. A warm breeze blew through the open window, and Emma-Jean imagined a crowd of skunks and raccoons and woodchucks listening raptly just outside, laughing along.

They were sipping tea when Vikram left the table to take a phone call. Emma-Jean's mother refilled their teacups, and began describing the garden she and Emma-Jean were planning for the backyard. Henri was peacefully asleep on her mother's shoulder, curled up against her glossy braid. Emma-Jean stifled a yawn. She too was extremely tired. Perhaps her crush on Will was sapping her energy.

"Why don't you go to sleep, Emma-Jean?" her mother said. "It's getting late."

Ms. Wright looked at her watch and gasped.

"Ten thirty! Where did the time go?"

Emma-Jean's mother looked around at the serving bowls and plates, scraped clean but for chicken bones and apricot pits. "I think we ate it," she said, much to the amusement of both Ms. Wright and Emma-Jean.

Emma-Jean stood up and said a reluctant good night. She did not like to leave such fine company, but she would need to be energized for tomorrow morning, when she would begin her investigation of the nine left-handed boys.

She had just finished brushing her teeth when she realized that in her state of fatigue, she had forgotten

Henri, who would be most perturbed if she went to sleep without wishing him sweet dreams. She went downstairs and was heading toward the dining room when Vikram's voice caught her attention. Something in his tone caused her to pause just outside the kitchen doorway. He was facing away from Emma-Jean, his phone pressed tightly to his ear.

"It's an incredible honor for me, Dr. Markt," he was saying.

Emma-Jean crept closer. Who was Dr. Markt? Emma-Jean had never heard Vikram mention this name before.

"No, I've never been to California, but I hear it is beautiful," he continued.

California? Who was inviting Vikram to California?

"Teaching at Stanford has been a dream for me for as long as I can remember."

Stanford University?

" . . . no, I haven't spread the news to anyone."

Emma-Jean suddenly felt chilled, though the house was very warm.

"Dr. Markt, thank you very much," Vikram said.

Emma-Jean crept away from the doorway and hurried back up to her room. Her fatigue had disappeared. She was now in a state of alarm, her eyes open wide, her breathing shallow and rapid.

Vikram was leaving them?

This question spun around her head, around and around until the words lost their meaning. Henri fluttered through the doorway. He sensed her distress and took up a position on her headboard. He stood up very straight and puffed out his chest.

Emma-Jean took her quilt from the foot of her bed and wrapped it around her shoulders. Her father had sewn it for her when she was born, and there had been only a short period in her life when it had not been on her bed. When Vikram's mother had her heart attack, Emma-Jean had hidden the quilt in Vikram's Pittsburgh Steelers duffel bag, hopeful that it would comfort him on the plane as he crossed two oceans to be by his mother's side.

Emma-Jean had been concerned that the quilt might not survive the trip; its edges were torn and fraying, badly in need of repair. But Vikram brought the quilt back to her not simply intact but transformed. The tattered patches had been removed. In their place were hundreds of tiny squares of sari silk, sewn carefully together by Vikram's mother as she regained her strength in the cardiac unit of Mumbai's Bhagwati Hospital.

Emma-Jean ran her fingers across the quilt's bright border as she considered this deeply disturbing turn of events. How could Vikram leave them? How could he plot his departure without telling Emma-Jean or her mother?

The dazzling colors of the silk seemed to light a pathway in Emma-Jean's mind, and before long she had an answer:

Love.

As her mother had said, true love was one of life's most powerful forces. In fairy tales, love could rouse a princess from death, or turn a frog into a prince. Love inspired poets to write and painters to paint and knights to perform their most heroic deeds.

But it was also true that love's power was unpredictable. Emma-Jean had heard the term "madly in love." Now she understood its meaning. Vikram was so deeply in love with her mother that he had temporarily lost his senses. He could not be trusted to make rational decisions.

Emma-Jean stood up, gripped by a sense of urgency. Luckily, her crush on Will Keeler had not significantly diminished her powers of logical thinking. She sat down at her desk, turned on her computer, and devised a plan of action.

She recalled the name of the person Vikram was speaking to: Dr. Markt. It took just a moment to locate him on the Stanford University website: Dr. David H. Markt, chairman of the department of microbiology and immunology. Emma-Jean read his impressive biography, which highlighted his laboratory work on smallpox and other pathogens. She studied his picture, focusing on his warm brown eyes. He seemed to regard her with curiosity and perhaps even a hint of understanding.

It took some time for Emma-Jean to compose a letter that achieved the appropriate tone. By the time she had finished, the sun had risen in the sky, and the smell of coffee and curried eggs filled their house.

"Emma-Jean?" her mother said, peering into the room. She was wearing Emma-Jean's father's faded terry-cloth robe and gripping a large mug of coffee. "You're looking very focused for so early in the morning."

Emma-Jean quickly closed out her computer screen; there was no need for her mother to discover Vikram's misguided plan.

"I'm just finishing a project," she said.

"It must be important," her mother said, taking a sip of coffee.

"It is urgent," Emma-Jean replied.

"Everything under control?" her mother said.

"I have done all I can."

"You always do," her mother said, smiling as she headed toward her bedroom.

Emma-Jean waited until she heard the rush of her mother's shower, and then reopened the file and printed out her letter.

Dr. David H. Markt
Stanford University
Chairman, Department of
Immunology and Microbiology
Fairchild Building
300 Pasteur Drive
Stanford, California 94305

Dear Dr. Markt,

I understand that you have hired Vikram
Adwani to join your faculty in the department of
immunology and microbiology at Stanford University.
It is understandable that you would wish for Vikram
to join your department because he is a man of
outstanding character and keen intelligence. And
if you admire his work with DNA, you will be most
impressed with what he can do with some curry and
garlic.

Unfortunately, it is not possible for Vikram to
work at Stanford. While Stanford is one of the finest
universities in the world, it is 3,000 miles away from
my mother, Elizabeth Lazarus, who is the love of

Vikram's life. I regret that Vikram did not consider this before accepting your offer. I have concluded that Vikram's love for my mother has made it difficult for him to think clearly. As perhaps you know, love can make people behave in irrational ways.

I have read about your work on smallpox and find it very fascinating. I hope you take the appropriate precautions with these dangerous pathogens, and wash your hands vigorously before eating your lunch.

Sincerely,
Emma-Jean Lazarus

Of course, there was no guarantee that the letter would resolve this matter. But Emma-Jean was hopeful. She sensed that Dr. Markt, a man of science, would see the logic in her message. And certainly Vikram would come to appreciate her intervention at this critical juncture in his life.

After all, there were many prestigious universities in the world. But there was only one Elizabeth Lazarus.

Chapter 15

All day in school, Colleen just kept getting Colleen-er and Colleen-er.

Like in her classes, she usually kept her hand down because even if she was sure of the answer, who knew what could fly out of her mouth? But now she couldn't stop herself. In science she raised her hand so many times that Mr. Petrowski started calling her Dr. Pomerantz, which everyone thought was really funny, and not in a mean way.

Between classes she usually waited for Kaitlin because Colleen didn't like walking through the halls alone. But now she realized she wasn't alone. Everywhere she looked there were people smiling at her. And whenever she saw Brandon or Will they would yell, "Hey Collcakes!" which for some reason felt really flattering.

But the weirdest of all was what happened after lunch.

For the second day in a row, Laura made them go out and dance. Usually dancing with Laura was torture because the moves were impossible and Colleen was a complete spaz. But today everything felt different. Colleen *wanted* to dance, to jump and leap and twirl all around. And so she did!

She jumped as high as she could and leaped like a ballerina and spun around until she felt dizzy. Valerie started to giggle and so did Colleen. She never knew dancing could actually be fun!

But then Laura started yelling.

"Colleen!" she said. "Those aren't the moves! What are you doing?"

"I'm just having fun," Colleen said.

"Well, you look like a complete dork," Laura yelled. "Pay attention!"

Laura shook her head and fluttered her eyes and

started showing the moves again. Colleen's friends followed along. But Colleen just stood there.

"Colleen!" Laura yelled. "Are you listening?"

Colleen *was* listening, but not to Laura. Someone was whispering in her ear.

Her boy was telling her something.

Walk away.

Really?

Just walk away.

"You know what?" Colleen said suddenly. "I'm going to take a break."

"What are you doing?" Kaitlin whispered.

"Are you okay?" Michele said.

"I'm fine," Colleen said. "I just . . . I just don't really want to do this anymore." And she walked away, like she'd always dreamed of doing, all those times when Laura made her feel like a shaky little dog who'd made a mess on the rug. She'd pictured this moment in her mind so many times, how she would walk slowly with her chin up, how her hair would fly behind her and her little bead earrings would jingle softly in her ears.

And that's exactly how it happened.

Colleen sat down on a bench and she felt her boy sit down right next to her. Colleen leaned against him, and she felt peaceful and strong, like she felt sometimes in church. She looked over at her friends, who were staring at her like she'd sprouted wings, which was sort of how she felt.

And a minute later, the most amazing thing: Valerie came walking over.

"I'm tired too," she said, plopping down on the bench and putting her head on Colleen's shoulder.

Michele came next, and then finally Kaitlin. They all squeezed in next to Colleen and her boy.

They sat there for a minute, and then Valerie started to giggle, very softly.

"Oh my God, I can't believe that just happened," she said.

"What do you think she'll do to us?" Kaitlin asked nervously.

They all peeked over at Laura, and Colleen expected her to be glaring at them. But she'd grabbed two other girls and was showing them her famous high kick.

She'd forgotten all about Colleen and her friends.

And suddenly Colleen understood the secret of Laura: She didn't care about anything or anyone, only herself. Colleen had always wished that she could be like that.

But now Colleen was getting a different idea.

That it wasn't bad to care. That you *had* to care— about people, about being nice, about having friends, about the boy out there who liked you best of all.

Because if you didn't care, then what was the point?

Colleen looked at her amazing friends. She felt so happy.

But then Valerie pointed across the blacktop and laughed.

"Look at Emma-Jean!" she said.

Emma-Jean was sitting on her favorite bench, under that huge crooked tree she loved. But now Emma-Jean wasn't staring up at the tree, like she usually did. She was looking over at the basketball court, at Will Keeler. She had her hand on her heart and this look on her face, this dreamy look.

"She's obsessed with him!" Kaitlin said.

"Poor Will!" Michele said, putting her hand over her mouth and cracking up.

Everyone started to giggle, except for Colleen.

"What's funny about Emma-Jean liking Will?" Colleen said.

Everyone looked at Colleen, and they tried to stop laughing, but they were still smiling.

"It's . . . cute is all," Valerie said, which was so wrong and everyone knew it. Emma-Jean was lots of great things—brilliant, gorgeous, clean. But Emma-Jean was never, ever cute.

"Emma-Jean should go to the dance with Will," Colleen said.

"Oh Coll, that's so ridiculous!" Valerie said, stamping her foot.

"No way!" Michele said.

"You're totally crazy if you think Will Keeler would go to the Spring Fling with Emma-Jean Lazarus," Kaitlin said. "You're dreaming!"

Maybe Colleen *was* dreaming. But was that so bad? How many amazing things had started out as dreams? Lightbulbs? Strawberry ice cream? Hamsters? You don't think those were dreams first?

"And Laura is going to ask him," Kaitlin said.

"She's going to ask him any second," Michele said. "You know that!"

"Why should I care about Laura?" Colleen said.

Colleen's cheeks felt hot, like she'd said a dirty word.

"Coll . . ." Kaitlin said. "That's not like you, to say something like that."

"Well, it's the truth," Colleen said, in a voice that was soft but strong, kind of like Ms. Wright's.

Her friends all looked at one another. Nobody said anything for a minute.

"I guess it would be kind of amazing if Emma-Jean went with Will," Valerie said.

Michele nodded.

"Anything's possible," Colleen said.

Her boy thought so too.

Chapter 16

Over the next two days, Emma-Jean made steady progress in her search for Colleen's admirer. Through patient observation and astute analysis, she was able to eliminate five left-handed boys from the list, three because they were going to the Spring Fling with other girls and two because they were absent on Monday, when the note was delivered to Colleen's locker.

That left only four boys: Dylan Dreyfuss, Aki Bofinger, Barry Lee, and Andrew Dinger. It pleased Emma-Jean to note that all were upstanding members of the William Gladstone community. She had harbored some concern that the admirer might be unsuitable for Colleen in some way. Regrettably, there were some boys in the seventh grade who could not be counted on for courtly companionship.

There had been a particularly unfortunate episode at the leprechaun dance this past March. Toward the end of the evening, Brandon Mahoney and several of his more rambunctious cohorts had commandeered the dance floor, stripped off their shirts, and banged their bare stomachs together like walruses competing for mates. Several girls had run shrieking from the cafeteria, and Mr. Tucci, the principal, had corralled the boys into the office and detained them until the dance was over.

Emma-Jean was confident that none of these four left-handed boys would engage in such an ungentlemanly display.

With only four boys to observe, Emma-Jean's job became much more manageable, and she could shift to the next phase of her investigation: surveillance of Colleen's locker. She had identified an ideal observation post: a utility room located across the hall from Colleen's locker. The room was kept unlocked, and the door had a small window through which Emma-Jean could watch.

As for missing her classes, that was not a problem. She wrote a general memo to all of her teachers explaining that she was working on an independent study project that would require her to miss classes for several days. Due to her impeccable academic record and unblemished disciplinary file, none of her teachers had questioned her plan.

Emma-Jean stood watch throughout Friday, taking just a short break to eat her lunch with her friends and enjoy a few moments of fresh air on the blacktop. She also did some light calisthenics to keep her muscles from cramping. She was performing a stretching maneuver when suddenly the door to the utility room swung open. Though she had permission to be out of classes, she had not specified that she would be spending her time in the utility room, which was marked with a sign that said "No Admittance." It was thus a relief when the doorway filled with the large figure of Mr. Johannsen.

He stepped back in alarm when he saw Emma-Jean.

"You almost gave me a heart attack there, missy," he said. "I thought you were a grizzly waiting to pounce."

"Mr. Johannsen, you know there are no grizzly bears in Connecticut," she said, quickly closing the door behind him.

"You got me there," he said, smoothing what was left of his fluffy white hair.

He eyed her with some concern.

"Everything a-okay here?" he said. "Kids giving you trouble?"

"No," said Emma-Jean, who found it perplexing that Mr. Johannsen so frequently asked her this question. Of course she wished there was less locker slamming and shrieking between classes, and more vigilant toilet flushing in the girls' room. But none of that was terribly troubling.

"Then mind if I ask what you're doing standing next to my water heater?" Mr. Johannsen asked.

"I am performing surveillance on Colleen's locker," Emma-Jean said.

"You are, are you?" Mr. Johannsen said.

"Yes," Emma-Jean said. "I am."

"Mind if I ask why?"

Emma-Jean hesitated for a moment, but then decided that Mr. Johannsen, who had flown top-secret missions during the Vietnam War, could be trusted with the classified details about Colleen's secret admirer.

"A boy left an anonymous note in Colleen's locker," Emma-Jean explained. "She has asked me to find him so that she can invite him to the Spring Fling."

"Ah, the Spring Fling," Mr. Johannsen said. "I'm afraid I'll be missing that one. The grandsons are coming in that weekend. We're having a little family celebration. For my retirement, you know. It's coming up fast."

"Yes, I know," said Emma-Jean, frowning at the mention of Mr. Johannsen's imminent departure, which she anticipated with dismay. She understood that after thirty-four years of service, Mr. Johannsen was ready to trade his mops and brooms for his fly-fishing pole. But Mr. Johannsen was one of the most important members of the William Gladstone staff. He was also one of Emma-Jean's closest friends. She could not imagine her days at school without him.

"Now hear this," Mr. Johannsen said, eyeing her from beneath his unruly eyebrows. "No need for the long face. I won't be here every day, that's true. But if you need me, you call me and I'll come running. You know that, right?"

It was difficult to picture the portly and arthritic Mr. Johannsen running for more than a few paces. But Emma-Jean understood his meaning: that they would always be friends. And besides, since Mr. Johannsen had a reliable car, running would not likely be necessary.

"Yes," she said. "I do know that."

"I'm glad you've got that straight," he said. He smiled at Emma-Jean, his familiar lopsided smile.

"I hope you're going to the dance," he said.

"That is unlikely."

"And why not?" Mr. Johannsen said.

"I don't enjoy dances," she said.

"You seemed to have fun at the last one," Mr. Johannsen said.

Emma-Jean thought back on the leprechaun dance—the uncomfortable heat in the cafeteria, the floor sticky with spilled soda, the pulsating music that pounded against her eardrums. How her friends had stood around her, how they made her laugh trying to coax her onto the dance floor.

Yes, it had been an enjoyable evening overall.

"I have nobody suitable to ask," Emma-Jean said.

"Nobody?"

"I would consider attending with Will Keeler, but he is likely going with someone else."

"He is, is he?"

"Yes. It is expected that Laura Gilroy will ask him."

"Laura Gilroy, eh," he said, shaking his head.

"Yes, Laura Gilroy."

They stood together for a moment as the water heater gurgled behind them, then Mr. Johannsen opened the door, which had a pronounced squeak.

"Okay then," Mr. Johannsen said, inspecting the door's hinges. "I'll see if I might be able to fix this little problem, missy."

After Mr. Johannsen left, Emma-Jean wondered what problem he was referring to.

Most likely it was the squeaky door.

Chapter 17

Colleen was in Spanish, where she was supposed to be learning about the customs of the indigenous people of Belize. But all she could think about was Kaitlin.

Why was she acting so strange?

It wasn't just today, Colleen realized. It had been going on all week. Since right around the time Colleen had found the note. Colleen wondered if Kaitlin's allergies were bothering her, or if she was worried about her cat Monty, who was thirteen and not getting any younger.

But no, that couldn't be it.

Colleen didn't want to be paranoid, but it was

almost like Kaitlin was mad at her. What had she done wrong?

"Señorita Pomerantz?"

"Sorry, Señora!" Colleen said.

"Consiga su cabeza de las nubes, señorita!" Señora Weingart said.

What was she saying?

A few of the smarter kids started to giggle.

"Sorry?" Colleen said.

Señora Weingart walked over and ruffled Colleen's hair.

"Get your head out of the clouds," she said softly.

Usually when this happened, Colleen wanted to click her pen and disappear in a puff of pink smoke and Wild at Heart perfume. But now Colleen understood that Señora Weingart just wanted Colleen to learn Spanish so she could achieve her dreams and have a happy life.

And besides, maybe Señora Weingart was right. Colleen's head *was* in *las nubes!* With her boy!

Colleen looked over at Kaitlin, who was sitting four rows away. Colleen and Kaitlin weren't allowed to sit together in Spanish; Señora Weingart had separated them back in September because they were always whispering. But it didn't matter. Colleen and Kaitlin could have a whole conversation with a few raised eyebrows, flared nostrils, and halfway smiles. They could be a football field apart and Colleen would still know exactly what Kaitlin was thinking.

Except for now.

Kaitlin would hardly look at Colleen. And when she did, her face was as blank as the blackboard.

Something was wrong.

Really, really, wrong.

And then Colleen remembered a fascinating article from the February issue of *Teen Beauty* magazine, which she read each and every month, because that magazine could really get you thinking. And not just about hair conditioner and nail polish. Like this one article, called

Friend-tastic!
How to be the best friend you can be!

It included a quiz, with really thought-provoking questions like:

1 **Who would you call first if you won the lottery?**
  a. Your best friend
  b. Your mom
  c. Your boyfriend
  d. Your poodle

2 **Who is the first person you think of when you wake up in the morning, and the last person on your mind when you go to sleep?**
  a. Your best friend
  b. Your boyfriend
  c. Your aunt Gertrude
  d. Your goldfish, Sal

Colleen had taken the quiz because it was always good to learn more about your inner self. She was totally honest because she would never cheat on any quiz. She'd added up her points and had been so happy to have gotten a 99. According to *Teen Beauty*, Colleen was a friend-tastic friend. "You always put your friends first," wrote the author, Dr. Amber Smith. Colleen had been really proud.

But now Colleen had a horrible thought.

She had taken that quiz before she'd had her boy. What if she took it again right now? Would she answer the questions the same way? Would Kaitlin be the first person she called if she won the lottery? Was Kaitlin still the first person Colleen thought of before she went to bed and when she woke up each morning?

Or . . .

Colleen took a deep breath.

Was her head so far up in the clouds, with her boy, that she hardly thought about Kaitlin at all?

Dr. Amber Smith would be so ashamed. She was a really famous friendship-ologist and she probably knew all about girls like Colleen, girls who got so boy crazy that they dumped their best friends.

Colleen wanted to cry. She wasn't friend-tastic anymore. No.

She was a . . .

Friend-isaster.

No wonder Kaitlin was mad! No wonder she didn't want to come to the youth group party. No wonder she didn't want Emma-Jean looking for Colleen's boy and she was tired of talking about the Spring Fling, which was all Colleen wanted to talk about!

How did this happen? Colleen had to get a grip! Having a boy had made her totally lose sight of her priorities.

Now she gave herself an even more important quiz.

When Colleen was the only girl in the entire fifth grade to not make the travel soccer team, who gave Colleen a stuffed piglet with the sweetest smile in the world? When Colleen's dad moved away, who never left Colleen's side? Who never told a soul that Colleen's mom cried in the middle of the night? Who convinced Colleen that it wasn't her fault?

Answer to all of the above: Kaitlin.

And how had Colleen thanked Kaitlin for being the best friend ever?

By abandoning her for her boy.

Colleen tried to catch Kaitlin's eye. More than

anything, she needed just one look—a blink—to let her know that she could make things right. But Kaitlin was busy writing. And then Kaitlin stood up. She walked to the front of the room and took the bathroom pass. She glanced at Colleen just before she walked out.

Wait, had she meant to look at Colleen?

Was it a signal?

Did she want Colleen to follow her, so they could talk?

Colleen wasn't sure, but thought she'd better go after her just in case.

Colleen raised her hand.

Señora Weingart came over.

"Mi amiga . . ." Colleen whispered. *"Yo soy . . ."*

"Sí?"

Colleen searched her mind, which was swirling around . . .

What was the Spanish word for *friend-isaster*?

Chapter 18

Emma-Jean was still in the utility room when she heard footsteps approaching from the eastern end of the hallway. She held her breath, hoping to see Dylan or Barry or Aki or Andrew moving stealthily toward Colleen's locker. It occurred to her that she should have brought her camera, to capture the moment. It would be impressive to include photographic evidence when she presented her final report to Colleen.

But it was Kaitlin.

Emma-Jean was tempted to signal to her, to invite Kaitlin into her observation post and to reveal the details of her plan. Given Kaitlin's doubts about Emma-Jean's abilities, it might reassure her to see Emma-Jean so diligently working on Colleen's behalf. Perhaps she might even want to assist.

Emma-Jean was about to open the door, but something in Kaitlin's manner caused her to hesitate. She was walking very quickly, with her head down and her curls in front of her face, as though she wished to hide. And then Emma-Jean wondered what had brought Kaitlin to this end of the building. She had Spanish this period, with Colleen. The foreign language wing had a newly renovated girls' room and working water fountain. Kaitlin's locker was on the other side of the school. There was no reason Emma-Jean could think of for Kaitlin to be on this end of the school building.

Kaitlin had stopped right in front of the utility room. Emma-Jean dropped to her knees. Very slowly she rose up, balancing on the balls of her feet so she could peer through the window. She watched as Kaitlin reached into the back pocket of her blue jeans and extracted a folded piece of paper. She looked around, then fed the folded paper into the vents of Colleen's locker.

What was Kaitlin doing? Could it be . . .

The floor beneath Emma-Jean seemed to tilt, and Emma-Jean leaned heavily against the door to steady herself. But the door was not properly closed. Emma-Jean's weight caused it to fly open with a piercing shriek. She stumbled into the hallway, stopping just a few feet from where Kaitlin was standing.

"Emma-Jean!" Kaitlin gasped.

"What are you doing?" Emma-Jean said.

Kaitlin did not answer.

But as a single cell can reveal the DNA code of an entire organism, the look in Kaitlin's eyes told Emma-Jean everything she needed to know:

That there was no secret admirer, no left-handed boy yearning for Colleen, waiting for her to ask him to the Spring Fling.

Kaitlin had written the note.

And far more shocking was the fact that Emma-Jean hadn't realized this the moment Colleen first showed her the note. Because right now, all of the clues lined up in Emma-Jean's mind like signs along the highway: Kaitlin was left-handed, Kaitlin had been eating buttery popcorn just before Colleen discovered the note, Kaitlin often wore a Band-Aid on her right index finger to conceal the large wart that so embarrassed her.

And of course there was the note itself. Who else but Kaitlin would write that Colleen was "the best girl in the whole grade"? How many times had Emma-Jean seen Kaitlin turn to Colleen and exclaim "You're the best!"?

"It would have worked," Kaitlin said in a defeated whisper. "But you figured it out."

"No, I did not," Emma-Jean said. "I had no idea."

Kaitlin studied Emma-Jean for a moment, then she closed her eyes and shook her head.

"It doesn't matter," she said. "Colleen will never forgive me. She—"

"Forgive you for what?" said a high, quavering voice behind Emma-Jean.

Colleen seemed to have appeared out of thin air.

And now she stepped forward.

"What's this?" Colleen said, plucking the note that was still stuck in the vent of her locker. "What are you doing?"

"I'm really sorry, Coll," Kaitlin said, and then she fled down the hallway.

Colleen stared down at the folded note, holding it lightly in her fingers, as though it was very hot.

"It was Kaitlin?" Colleen said.

Emma-Jean nodded.

"Were you in on it, Emma-Jean?" she said. "Did you know the whole time?"

"No," Emma-Jean said, in a voice that sounded curiously far away, as though she was speaking from deep within a cave. "I did not know, not until just a moment ago."

Colleen looked at Emma-Jean. And her look was not one of hope and trust. Her eyes appeared cloudy, like windows on a misty day.

Colleen looked down at the floor, and tears splashed onto the tiles. Emma-Jean stepped forward, wishing to offer her some comfort. But Colleen turned and hurried away, leaving Emma-Jean in the hallway. And though she knew that the rooms around her were filled with boys and girls and teachers, Emma-Jean felt entirely alone.

Chapter 19

Dear Colleen,

I wrote the note to you.

I didn't do it as a joke or to be mean. I did it because I wanted you to know what an amazing person you are.

I never thought everything would get so out of control. I never ever wanted to hurt you. And I'm so, so, so sorry.

No matter what happens, I will always think of you as the best friend in the world.

Love,
Kaitlin

Colleen read and reread the note as she sat on a bench in the empty girls' locker room. By now the note was soggy from her tears, which poured down her face.

How had she been so stupid? She should have known that a boy would never write her a note! Her bird was probably laughing at her from his branch. He'd probably told all his friends, and probably now they were all giggling at Colleen, or whatever birds do when they think something is really funny.

She had been so wrong, about everything. And now any minute a huge sadness would come crashing over her. And it would last for days and days, like it had after the disaster with Laura. She wouldn't be Colleen-er anymore. Any minute, all those happy and brave and strong feelings would drain out of her heart. She hoped it wouldn't hurt too much.

She watched the clock on the wall, with the jumping second hand, tick-tock, tick-tock . . . She felt like Cinderella at 11:59 p.m, except that Colleen's mom would never let her wear a glass shoe, especially one with such a high heel.

Colleen closed her eyes, but the tears kept pouring down.

What would she do now? How would she face everyone? And what about the Spring Fling? While all of her friends were having the best night of their lives, Colleen would be home alone with her mom and her sock puppets.

Colleen sat on the bench, waiting for the sadness.

She waited.

And waited.

But nothing happened.

What was wrong? She looked up at the ceiling, expecting to see a dark cloud gathering above her. But the ceiling was bright white.

She wiped her eyes.

And a tiny speck of an idea flickered in her mind:

Maybe this wasn't so bad.

The idea disappeared for a minute, but then there it was, sparkling a little brighter.

Maybe she didn't have to be sad.

Of course she did. She should feel totally horrible and humiliated and lonely and stupid.

So why didn't she?

Because even though she was sitting here in the locker room, which smelled like old socks and bleach, some part of Colleen had been able to fly away up to that branch, where it was sunny, where the breeze blew softly into her face and dried her tears. Her bird wasn't there, because he was off doing something more important than laughing at Colleen, like looking for worms for his wife and babies. Colleen was up there by herself, looking down at the school, through the windows and down the hallway to the locker room. And she could see herself sitting there.

And sure, her eyes looked all puffed up and red from crying, and her bangs were mashed down against her forehead. But she didn't look so bad. She didn't look like her life was ruined. She looked like a girl who was a little sad and disappointed but who could, if she wanted, stand up, take a deep breath, wash her face, and go out there to find her best friend in the world and make things right.

Because nothing terrible had happened to Colleen. Nobody important had moved away. She hadn't hurt anyone and nobody had tried to make her into a big joke. In fact, wasn't the opposite kind of true? Hadn't Kaitlin written that secret admirer note because she wanted Colleen to feel better about herself, because Kaitlin *cared?*

And guess what? It had worked! The note had made Colleen Colleen-er. And now that she was Colleen-er, she could stay Colleen-er, if she wanted to.

She wanted to.

But could she do it?

She could try.

And so Colleen stood up. Her knees felt wobbly at first, but then stronger. She walked to the sink, washed her face, and fluffed up her bangs. She took a deep breath and looked at herself in the mirror. She smiled a little, a sad smile, but kind of brave too.

It felt like hours had passed, but only seven minutes had ticked by on the clock. If she hurried, she could maybe make it back to Spanish before the bell.

But wait!

She couldn't go just yet. There was something she needed to do before she headed out into the world.

Colleen had to say good-bye to her boy.

Chapter 20

Emma-Jean wasn't sure where to go after Colleen and Kaitlin left her, and so she returned to the utility room. She closed the door and sat down on the cold tiles. Her mind continued to race and she was sweating. She had the sense that the delicate equilibrium of the William Gladstone universe had been upset and that chaos lurked just outside. She remembered Colleen's grief in the aftermath of the ski trip, how she had yelled at Emma-Jean. *"Why would I want help from YOU?"* she had sobbed. *"Why are you even here?"*

Those were the last words that Emma-Jean had heard before she fell from the tree. She did not want to hear such words again.

And so she determined that she could stay in the utility room until the dismissal bell rang and the buses had rumbled away. She would then hurry through the empty halls and out the door, and run home to her room. The thought comforted her— Henri's velvety cheek against her own, the dogwood out her window, the smell of curry and garlic, her father's picture smiling out at her.

Yes, that's what she would do. She would get home. After that, well, she couldn't be sure what she would do. The situation was too unstable to make plans for the future.

The dismissal bell rang, and Emma-Jean heard the muffled pounding of hundreds of feet against the floor, the slamming of lockers, the giggles and hoots of her peers. And then she heard screaming.

"Oh my God! Oh my God!"

For a moment she thought it might be Colleen. But no, the timbre of Colleen's voice was not so shrill. And now it wasn't just one person screaming. It sounded like a whole crowd of girls screaming in panic.

"Ahhhh!"

"What happened!"

"No way!"

Emma-Jean scrambled to her feet. Something was seriously wrong in the seventh-grade wing, and Emma-Jean could not simply sit idly while a crisis unfolded. Her peers were clearly in need of assistance.

She flung open the door and rushed down the hall in the direction of the chorus of screams.

"Ahhhhhhh! Oh my God!"

Emma-Jean could see a crowd of girls huddled together, and Laura Gilroy's golden head in the center. But before she could get close, Colleen came bounding up to her. And she did not look panicked or distressed. She was smiling, and Kaitlin was right behind her, holding Colleen's hand.

"Everything is okay!" Colleen said.

Relief rushed over Emma-Jean with such force that tears came to her eyes. Colleen wrapped her arms around Emma-Jean, her thin arms holding her with surprising strength. Emma-Jean did not step back as she normally did when one of her friends became overly exuberant in their affections. She rested her hands lightly on Colleen's back and stood very still. She had the feeling that not even the strongest gust of wind could knock them down.

Finally the shrieks around them became too loud to ignore.

"What has happened?" Emma-Jean said as she and Colleen parted.

"You won't believe it," Kaitlin said. "You know Mr. Johannsen's grandson Carl? The one on TV?"

"Of course," Emma-Jean said.

"He's coming to town," said Colleen.

"Mr. Johannsen told me," Emma-Jean said. "There is a retirement party."

"Did he tell you he was going to invite Laura so she could meet Carl?" Kaitlin said.

"No," Emma-Jean said. "Why would he do that?"

Emma-Jean knew that Mr. Johannsen did not think highly of Laura, who was bossy and rude, even to staff members, and routinely threw her gum wrappers onto the floor.

What possible reason would he have for including her in a family celebration?

"He must know that Laura is such a big fan," Colleen suggested.

"But it makes no sense," Emma-Jean said.

"And it means Laura has to miss the Spring Fling," Kaitlin said.

"It does?" Emma-Jean said.

"Yes," Colleen said. "It's the same night!"

Of course it was. Mr. Johannsen had told her that.

"And everyone knows Laura is obsessed with Carl Johannsen," Kaitlin added.

Colleen nodded. "She'd do anything to meet him, so I guess . . ."

Colleen and Kaitlin continued to speculate about Laura, but Emma-Jean was no longer listening.

Because she understood exactly why her friend Mr. Johannsen had invited Laura to his party.

"I'll see if I might be able to fix this little problem, missy."

And indeed he had.

She stood very still, marveling at the afternoon's surprising twists and turns, at the unpredictable forces at work in the William Gladstone universe.

She looked at Colleen, who stood close to Kaitlin, her cheeks flushed with excitement as they chattered about Laura.

And suddenly Emma-Jean was struck by an idea, an idea so stunning and simple she couldn't imagine why she hadn't thought of it before. Her heart began to pound, and this time she knew exactly what it meant.

"I must go now," she said to Colleen and Kaitlin, rushing past them with barely a wave.

There was someone she needed to speak to without delay.

Chapter 21

Emma-Jean finally found Will Keeler in the empty cafeteria. He was kneeling in front of the vending machine, his entire arm stuck up through the machine's front slot.

"Are you caught?" said Emma-Jean, alarmed.

"Nah," Will said. "The machine ate my dollar. I just want my barbequed chips."

Emma-Jean took a dollar bill from her school-bag and fed it into the machine, punching in the correct code so that the desired bag dropped into Will's hand.

Will stood up. "Thanks," he said, ripping open the bag as he began to walk away. "See you later."

"Wait," Emma-Jean said. "I need to speak to you."

"Okay," Will said, tossing a chip into his mouth.

"Do you recall that I solved your problem with Mr. Petrowski and the missing chocolates?" Emma-Jean asked.

"Yeah," Will said. "You saved my butt."

"Do you recall what you said afterward?" Emma-Jean said.

Will chewed, his eyes thoughtful. "Thanks?" he said.

"Yes," Emma-Jean said. "But you also said that you owed me."

"Oh yeah," said Will. "I do. You really helped me out."

"Well, now there is something important you could do for me," said Emma-Jean.

"Okay," Will said. "Sure."

"Of course you are aware of the Spring Fling," Emma-Jean said.

Will appeared to get a chip stuck in his throat. He coughed and then swallowed hard.

"I would like to ask you," Emma-Jean continued, "if you are willing to go with—"

"No I can't," Will said quickly. "I hate dances, and I already told Laura I couldn't go, so I can't just show up with someone else."

"Laura Gilroy asked you to the Spring Fling?" Emma-Jean said with surprise.

"Like a month ago."

Emma-Jean shook her head, marveling anew at Laura's cunning.

"That is very interesting," she said.

Of course Laura would not publicize the details of her rejection, and she must have known that Will was too gallant to broadcast the truth. Emma-Jean tried to imagine the look on Laura's face when he declined her invitation. Had she pleaded with him? Had she rushed to the girls' room to cry as some other girls did when they were dejected?

Surprisingly, this image brought no satisfaction to Emma-Jean. She felt a tinge of pity for Laura, though it came and went quickly.

In any case, she would keep this information to herself.

"Laura is no longer concerned about the Spring

Fling," Emma-Jean said. "As you might have heard, she has another engagement that night. And so you are now free to attend."

Will's eyes moved searchingly around the room, as they did when Ms. Wright called on him to define a vocabulary word.

"Well, I guess I could do that," he said, "if that's what you really want me to do."

"You would be doing me a great favor if you would go with Colleen Pomerantz."

Will's eyes became very large.

"You don't . . . Colleen?" he said.

"She is a fine person," Emma-Jean said, "and a suitable companion for you. You are fortunate to have this opportunity."

"Really? Colleen wants to go with me?" Will said incredulously. "Are you sure?"

"I have not asked her specifically," Emma-Jean said.

"Then how do you know?" he said.

"Because I believe any girl in the seventh grade would be pleased to attend with you."

A pink flush appeared on Will's ruddy cheeks.

But then he smiled. "Nancy Freakin' Drew," he said. "Always working some angle."

"So you are willing to go with Colleen?"

"Sure, yeah, Colleen," he said. "Wow. That's pretty cool."

"Very good," Emma-Jean said.

Will crumpled up his bag of chips and tossed it across two tables into the garbage can.

He stepped up and put his hand on Emma-Jean's head, ruffling her hair.

"You really are a good kid," he said.

Emma-Jean nodded, relieved that Will was so amenable to her proposal.

And it was at that moment that Emma-Jean made an unexpected discovery:

Her crush on Will Keeler was over.

Though she was standing very close to Will, her heart was not fluttering. She felt none of the jittery agitation that had gripped her over the past two days whenever Will was nearby. What excitement she felt right now was for Colleen, her kind and generous friend, who would be most pleased to discover this surprising turn of events.

She leaned closer to Will to confirm that her crush had subsided completely. She was close enough to see the flecks of violet in his bright blue eyes. And yet she felt utterly calm.

There was no doubt. Her crush was over. Will was certainly an honorable person. But it was very clear to her now that they were not well suited for each other.

"What's the matter?" Will asked.

"Not a thing," said Emma-Jean with satisfaction and just the slightest wisp of disappointment. "Everything is as it should be."

Chapter 22

It always amazed Colleen, how your world could break apart into a thousand pieces, like a plate you dropped while emptying the dishwasher. And then somehow everything was put together again, and you couldn't even see the cracks or the glue. It hadn't taken long to make things right with Kaitlin. There was no huge talk, just a look and some tears and about a hundred hugs and they were back to normal. And with the news about Laura and Carl Johannsen, nobody was thinking about Colleen and her secret admirer. The whole thing was forgotten. Which was fine with Colleen.

Colleen and Kaitlin called their moms and said

they were walking into town to get ice cream.

"We need to celebrate," Colleen had said.

"What are we celebrating?" Kaitlin asked.

Colleen wondered. She wasn't going to the Spring Fling. She had no secret admirer.

Colleen shrugged. "Just everything!" she said, and of course Kaitlin understood exactly what she meant and gave her another big hug.

Kaitlin needed to use the girls' room before their walk into town. Colleen was waiting for her when Will came jogging up to her.

"Hey Collcakes," he said.

He was so sweet!

She wondered how he felt about Laura and Carl Johannsen. He didn't look too upset. He looked pretty happy, actually. And then it hit Colleen . . . Will wasn't going to the Spring Fling with Laura! And so now . . .

Without even thinking, Colleen grabbed Will's hand and blurted out, "Will you go to the Spring Fling with Emma-Jean?"

Will stared at her, and then he started to laugh.

"That's a good one," he said.

"What's so funny?" Colleen demanded.

Maybe Will wasn't sweet! Maybe he was mean and awful!

"Emma-Jean is a great person," Colleen said, crossing her arms.

Will stopped laughing. "I know that," he said.

"So go with her to the dance!" Colleen said, bouncing up and down. This was so exciting! See? *Anything* was possible!

"Emma-Jean doesn't want to go with me," Will said.

"Yes she does," Colleen said. "She totally does!"

Will shook his head. "No, I just talked to her."

"You did?" Colleen said. That was strange. Was Will making this up?

"She uh, she said I should go with someone else."

What was Will talking about? Did he think that Colleen was stupid? Did he think she didn't know Emma-Jean at all?

"Really," Colleen said, raising her chin and looking right at Will. "Who?"

Will smiled a little. "You."

Colleen blinked.

"What?"

"She said we were . . . what did she say? Oh yeah . . . suitable."

Oh gosh. Will couldn't have thought of that on his own. Only Emma-Jean would use that word.

What had Emma-Jean done? Did she really think that Will Keeler would go to the Spring Fling with *Colleen?* Even Emma-Jean should know better than that! Was she trying to ruin Colleen's life again?

She couldn't look at Will. This was so embarrassing! Didn't Emma-Jean ever learn?

But then she felt Will's hand on her shoulder, strong and soft at the same time.

And Colleen peeked up. Will was looking right into her eyes, looking at her in a way that nobody had ever looked at her before, not her mom or her friends or Piggy or even her boy. Colleen looked right back.

"Do you want to go with me, Colleen?" Will said in the most serious voice she'd ever heard. "Because I really want to go with you."

Colleen just stood there with her mouth wide open in shock. The roof of the school seemed to open over their heads, so that the sun was shining down on both of them. And her bird flew over, with all of his friends. And they were all singing together. . .

La, la, la
La, la, la
La, la, la
      la
        la
          la
            la
          la
        la
      LA!

Chapter 23

Over the next two weeks, Emma-Jean's friends focused on their preparations for the Spring Fling. They pored over fashion magazines at lunch and debated the merits of different hairstyles and nail polish hues. Kaitlin went to the doctor and had her wart removed. The slumber party was rescheduled for the weekend after the dance.

"And I have the best idea ever," Colleen said. "We'll do it at your house, Emma-Jean! That way your bird won't be lonely."

Emma-Jean agreed that it was an inspired solution, and she and Vikram had started working on a dinner menu that would go well with chocolate fondue.

She was pondering this and other pleasant matters on a warm Thursday afternoon when Vikram appeared at her door carrying a large box festooned with Indian postage stamps.

"It's from my mother," he said. "There is something in here for you."

Vikram placed the box on Emma-Jean's desk and took out a flat rectangular package wrapped in tissue. There was a short note taped to the top, written in Mrs. Adwani's distinctive dancing Hindi lettering.

It took Emma-Jean just a few minutes to decipher the words.

For you, Emma-Jean,
My son tells me you will
be attending a dance.
Wear this in good health
and joy.
Mrs. Prakesh Adwani
(Lata)

Emma-Jean unwrapped the package and discovered a seemingly endless bolt of bright orange silk edged with delicate crystal beads.

"It's very striking," Emma-Jean said, holding the fabric to her cheek. It was as soft as Henri. "Though I am not going to a dance."

"One day you will," Vikram said.

Emma-Jean nodded. She carefully folded the silk and held it to her chest.

"What else is in the box?" she asked.

"It's my cricket collection," Vikram said.

For an instant Emma-Jean imagined the dazzling spectacle of dozens of crickets hopping out of the box, filling her bedroom with their symphony of chirps. But of course she realized that Vikram was not referring to the cricket of the etymological world, but rather that of the sporting world, the baseball-like game that had captivated him since he was a small boy.

He opened the flaps and stared inside with reverence, like a pirate peering into a chest of long-buried gold. Emma-Jean looked over his shoulder, admiring the array of items—dozens of neatly bundled stacks of player cards, felt caps, team photographs and pennants.

Vikram reached into the box and brought out a long and bulky object wrapped in many layers of newspaper. He carefully stripped away the paper to reveal a cricket bat that was battered and grass-stained and emblazoned with an illegible signature scrawled in black marker.

"Donald Bradman's bat," he whispered.

"Who was he?" Emma-Jean said.

Vikram looked at her with surprise. "He is one of the most famous men in the world," Vikram said. "He was a cricket player, a legend."

"Why did he give you his bat?"

Vikram seemed amused by this comment.

"He did not. My grandfather did. He gave it to me just before he died. It is worth a small fortune now. My mother sent it because I have finally decided to sell it. I am planning to take a major step in my life."

A feeling of dread came over Emma-Jean. The weeks had passed with no mention of the job at Stanford University; Emma-Jean had been hopeful that her letter to Dr. Markt had been effective. But now it seemed that in fact Dr. Markt had not received her letter, or he had received it and not heeded Emma-Jean's warning about Vikram's precarious state of mind.

"I have not told a soul about this," Vikram continued. "Not even your mother."

Emma-Jean took a deep breath.

"I am aware of your plan," she said.

"Really?" Vikram said with surprise.

"Yes I am," Emma-Jean said. "And I must tell you that I am utterly against it."

Vikram blinked, as though startled by a clap of thunder.

"I'm surprised to hear you say this," Vikram said. "I expected—"

"You are not thinking clearly," Emma-Jean explained. "You are madly in love with my mother. Your judgment has become clouded."

"Clouded?"

"The plan is misguided," Emma-Jean said. "To

move to California. To teach at Stanford. I heard you speaking on the phone to Dr. Markt. I have already written to him. I have explained the situation. I had hoped—"

"You wrote to Dr. Markt?" Vikram interrupted.

Emma-Jean nodded.

"Well, that explains a few things," he said, shaking his head.

And then Vikram did something quite peculiar. He began to chuckle. And it occurred to Emma-Jean that perhaps Vikram's mental state was even more unbalanced than she had feared.

"Did you by any chance tell him I liked to cook with curry?"

"Yes," Emma-Jean said.

Vikram's laughter grew stronger until it seemed to fill the room around them and spill out the open window to echo through the streets.

Emma-Jean watched in alarm, wondering if she should call her mother at work.

Finally Vikram stopped laughing. He patted his chest and cleared his throat.

"Emma-Jean," he said. "I am not moving to California. I have been invited to lead a seminar, over the summer. Your mother and I thought you could both join me for a couple of weeks. We were waiting to tell you, until we had it all planned. It was to be a surprise."

Emma-Jean opened her mouth to respond, but somehow all of her words had disappeared. Perhaps they had been carried out the window by the force of Vikram's laughter.

"I had wondered why Dr. Markt was so curious about my cooking . . . and about you."

"Me?"

Vikram nodded. "He will be in Connecticut next week, visiting his mother. He asked if he could come here, for dinner. He specifically asked if you would be here. And he said something very peculiar . . . He said to let you know that he would wash his hands very well before dinner. He hung up before I could ask him what he meant by that."

Vikram looked searchingly at Emma-Jean, and his expression grew stern.

"You should have spoken to me," Vikram said quietly. "It is not a good idea to be writing letters to people you don't know. Dr. Markt obviously has a good sense of humor, but you could have . . ."

But then his eyes softened. He picked up Emma-Jean's hand and held it to his chest.

"We can discuss that another time. What I wanted to tell you has nothing to do with California or Stanford," Vikram said. "I'm selling the bat because I plan to buy your mother a ring."

Vikram held her hand tighter.

"Emma-Jean," Vikram said. "I want to ask your mother to marry me."

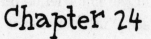

Chapter 24

Colleen had always dreamed that one day she would go to a fancy ball in a pink dress with the nicest boy in the world. Dreams really do come true!

Well, maybe not *exactly* true. At her dream ball, Colleen's mom hadn't been a chaperone.

But when your dream came true, you shouldn't be picky about the details. They needed chaperones at the Spring Fling, and her mom seemed excited to be coming along. She'd even bought a new blouse, with pink flowers on it, and put on lipstick. She looked pretty! Colleen was happy they were going out together, that neither one of them was home alone with the sock puppets.

She was nervous that her mom would hover around her all night, but as soon as they walked inside she gave Colleen a little kiss and went off to help set up the refreshments.

Colleen could see her friends on the dance floor. But she didn't see Will. They never said where they would meet. What if he didn't come? What if he ignored her? What if her breath smelled like egg salad?

She started to get her old panicky feeling. But then someone seemed to be right there with her telling her to calm down.

Her boy! He was here! Even though they'd said good-bye, he was here tonight, just in case Colleen needed him. And now he was telling her that of course Will was coming. He reminded her that she and Will had been talking about the dance every day for weeks. And her breath couldn't smell like egg salad, because she purposely hadn't eaten it for three days.

And then she felt someone's hands over her eyes, for real, and a funny voice whispering in her ear.

"Collcakes."

And Colleen grabbed Will's wrists and turned around and they both laughed. And oh my gosh he looked so cute!

Oh no! What if her boy got jealous of Will?

But no, of course he wasn't jealous. That's not how it was with Colleen and her boy. The only thing he'd ever wanted was for Colleen to be happy. And now Colleen had the feeling that he would always be there for her, somewhere, in case she needed him.

"Let's go dance!" she shouted to Will over the music.

"I hate dancing!" Will shouted back.

"No you don't!" said Colleen.

"Okay, maybe I don't," Will laughed.

And they ran over to the dance floor, where all her friends were already dancing. They made room for Will and Colleen and they were all dancing together. And Colleen closed her eyes for a few seconds because she knew this was one of those precious moments that she'd want to remember for her whole life.

They had just finished dancing when she saw Emma-Jean.

How amazing that she was here! And she looked so gorgeous in orange. But, well, maybe for the next dance Colleen's mom could show her how to sew that pretty piece of material into a real dress.

"Look!" Colleen said, pointing to Emma-Jean. "She's here!"

"Who?" Will said.

"Emma-Jean!"

"I can't believe it!" Kaitlin said.

"That's amazing!" Valerie said.

Emma-Jean was standing there, looking around in that Emma-Jean-ish way, like she was studying them for a science project.

"Emma-Jean!" Colleen called, waving the hand that Will wasn't holding.

"Emma-Jean!" Kaitlin called.

"Emma-Jean!" Valerie and Michele called together.

They all started to laugh.

"She's in her own world," Will said, but not in a mean way. It was like he understood how it was with Emma-Jean.

"Okay, on three," Colleen said. "We'll all yell together."

They all huddled together, Valerie and Jeremy, Michele and Leo, Kaitlin and Neil, and Colleen and Will.

Colleen and Will?

This was way better than any dream.

"Okay," said Colleen as loudly as she could. "One! Two! Three!"

And they all took deep breaths and shouted together across the cafeteria.

"Emma-Jean!"

Chapter 25

The decision to attend the Spring Fling had been made just that morning, when Ms. Wright had phoned Emma-Jean's mother to say that the PTA still needed some chaperones.

Emma-Jean had listened as she ate her oatmeal, and when her mother hung up, Emma-Jean said, "Perhaps we should go."

The words had come out unexpectedly.

"Really?" Emma-Jean's mother said. "You want to go to the dance?"

"Yes," Emma-Jean said, before she could consider the question too deeply.

"And you want Vikram and me to go too?"

"Vikram has never been to a dance," Emma-Jean said. "It is one of his regrets."

"I didn't realize that."

"It's true," Emma-Jean said. "And that is why we should go."

It all seemed rational enough, Emma-Jean thought.

Apparently her mother agreed, because she smiled and grabbed Emma-Jean's hand and said, "Let's go tell Vikram!"

They arrived at the dance more than thirty minutes late, having been delayed by the challenge of arranging Emma-Jean's sari. After an hour of fruitless folding and wrapping and tucking of the orange silk, Emma-Jean's mother had placed a call to Mrs. Adwani, who had not been the least bit annoyed to be awakened at 3:35 a.m. Mumbai time. Despite the early hour, Mrs. Adwani provided coherent instructions to Emma-Jean's mother, who then adeptly wrapped the sari around Emma-Jean's body and draped it over her shoulder. The results were quite fetching.

When they arrived at the school, they found Ms. Wright standing in the doorway of the gym.

"Here you are!'" she said. "And look how stunning you are, Emma-Jean!"

"Thank you," said Emma-Jean said, confirming that her sari was secure. "You look stunning as well."

Indeed, Ms. Wright looked especially lovely in a blue dress, which swished gracefully around her knees. Emma-Jean made a mental note to suggest to Ms. Wright that she wear this dress on Wednesday night, to the dinner Vikram was preparing in honor of Dr. Markt. It had been Emma-Jean's idea to include Ms. Wright in the dinner, and Vikram and her mother had readily concurred.

"She loves Vikram's puran-poli," her mother had said, referring to Vikram's mother's signature dish, a stuffed bread that Vikram would be making for the dinner.

But Emma-Jean had her secret reason for inviting Ms. Wright, a reason that had nothing at all to do with the puran-poli: She had come to see that the illustrious scientist and her esteemed teacher would make an excellent couple.

Over the past two weeks, Vikram had shared

with Emma-Jean some compelling details about Dr. Markt—that he traveled to Connecticut frequently, that he played the mandolin, that he was unmarried. These facts, combined with Dr. Markt's demonstrated intelligence and sense of humor, had led Emma-Jean to conclude that he had many of the qualities that Ms. Wright was looking for.

Emma-Jean had not revealed any of this to Ms. Wright, who might become nervous if she knew she could soon be meeting her future husband. Besides, Emma-Jean could do no more than arrange their meeting. She knew better than to think she could control the unpredictable forces of love. Still, her hopes were high.

Now Ms. Wright linked arms with Emma-Jean's mother.

"I need to take these tardy chaperones to their post," she said.

"Do you want to come with us?" her mother said.

Emma-Jean shook her head. "I will find my friends."

Vikram waved and her mother blew her a kiss.

The small diamond on her mother's engagement ring seemed to wink at Emma-Jean as they disappeared into the crowd.

Emma-Jean slowly made her way across the gym. She passed Mr. Petrowski, who was standing behind a pile of mats. He was engrossed in conversation with a plump woman wearing a bright flowered blouse. It took Emma-Jean a moment to recognize Colleen's mother.

"And next thing I knew they gave me a new Cadillac Escalade," Mr. Petrowski was saying.

"That is a remarkable story!" said Mrs. Pomerantz, her hand fluttering across her chest like Colleen's did when she was excited.

"I'm glad you think so. I've got a million stories," Mr. Petrowski said, standing up straighter and adjusting his glasses.

"Well, I for one would enjoy hearing them."

"Where to start?" Mr. Petrowski said, and they both laughed.

Emma-Jean smiled to herself. Love really was in the air, she realized. Perhaps it wasn't too late for Mr. Petrowski after all.

Emma-Jean walked to the back of the gym and stood against the wall. She admired the festive decorations and the girls and boys dressed in their finery. Two boys were standing next to her. The closer one was Brandon Mahoney, who looked surprisingly presentable in his buttoned-down shirt and pressed pants.

"This dance kind of stinks," he said to his friend. "Nobody wants to do anything fun."

She followed Brandon's gaze across to the dance floor, where Will and Colleen were standing together.

Emma-Jean looked at Brandon, and their eyes met. Emma-Jean girded herself for one of Brandon's unkind smirks, or for him to whisper an unclever pun based on her last name. But he nodded to her, rather cordially. And for the first time she noted something in Brandon's face—the determined set of his eyes, an almost regal arch of his nose. Could it be that Brandon Mahoney looked a bit like . . . George Washington?

Oh no.

Emma-Jean hurried away. She would be sure to avoid Brandon in the coming weeks, or until she could be entirely sure that the epidemic of spring fever had passed.

As she walked through the crowd, she heard something, a rhythmic chorus, chanting her name.

Emma-Jean!

Emma-Jean!

It was her friends.

Emma-Jean!

Emma-Jean!

She looked at them with surprise. They were smiling at her, and waving, beckoning for her to join them.

And then a warm feeling came over her, though it seemed to have nothing to do with the temperature in the gym. The feeling came from within her, and it grew stronger as she made her way toward her friends, who continued to call her name.

Emma-Jean!

Emma-Jean!

Their voices swirled around her, encircling her like the soft silk of her sari, lighting the air around her like the sparkle of her father's eyes.

As she stepped into their midst, she felt their hands on her shoulders, the girls' kisses brushing her cheeks. She closed her eyes and smiled. And for a moment she couldn't hear anything, not the music or the giggles or the shouts.

All she could hear was her own poetic heart, beating steady and true, echoing with possibilities.

DISCUSSION QUESTIONS

1. Do you think it's possible to keep yourself completely separate from the people around you? How has Emma-Jean kept her distance from her fellow classmates, and what happens to change that?

2. How does the way Emma-Jean observes the world around her and thinks about situations differ from the way her classmates do? How does her unique perspective help her, and how does it make things more difficult for her?

3. What does Colleen think is important? How does her attitude toward people and things affect what happens in each story?

4. What do you think about the way Emma-Jean handles the problems of her classmates? Do you think she deals with the issues that come up in the right way? What information does she miss because of the way she thinks? How would you handle these situations?

5. What do you think of Laura? How do her actions affect the people around her? What is the difference in the reactions that Emma-Jean and Colleen have to Laura?

6. How do Emma-Jean and Colleen influence each other's reactions to different situations, and how have they changed as a result of their friendship?

7. Why does Emma-Jean Lazarus think that Will Keeler is an honorable person? Do you agree?

8. What are Colleen's and Emma-Jean's reactions to the thought of having crushes? How do they understand what a "crush" is, and what are their thoughts on having a crush?

9. How does Colleen act after getting a secret love letter? How does her perspective on situations change as a result? How does she react when the secret of the love letter isn't a secret anymore? What are the positive and negative things that come from Colleen's secret love letters?

10. What does Colleen think it means to be a good friend? How is she a good friend? How is Emma-Jean a good friend? What do they learn about friendship from each other and from the situations in the story?

SCHOLASTIC JUNIOR CLASSICS

The
Pied Piper

Retold from Robert Browning
by Ellen Miles

SCHOLASTIC INC.

New York   Toronto   London   Auckland   Sydney

Mexico City   New Delhi   Hong Kong   Buenos Aires

No part of this publication may be reproduced in whole or in part, or stored in a retrieval system, or transmitted in any form or by any means, electronic, mechanical, photocopying, recording, or otherwise, without written permission of the publisher. For information regarding permission, write to Scholastic Inc., Attention: Permissions Department, 557 Broadway, New York, NY 10012.

Copyright © 2002 by Ellen Miles.

All rights reserved. Published by Scholastic Inc. SCHOLASTIC and associated logos are trademarks and/or registered trademarks of Scholastic Inc.

ISBN 0-439-43653-2

12 11 10 9 8 7 6 5 4 3 2 1   2 3 4 5 6 7/0
Printed in the U.S.A.   40
First Scholastic printing, September 2002